Piper Nuelle

Death's Carousel

Beta Reader Praises for Death's Carousel...

~ A modern take on *'Carrie'*, just without the superpower of Telekinesis... JP

~ A triumph of showing what can happen to people when pushed too far... IG

~ An Indie masterpiece of how bullies always get their comeuppance... Anon

~ A strangely, wonderful thrilling ride of horror, with a musical twist added into the mix... BM

~ Never push a woman to the brink, you never know what horror's they may bring to the table... JG

Thanks to my Beta readers for reading my story and helping me make it the best it can be... xo Piper xo

Piper Nuelle...

Piper Nuelle is an Author and Blogger from Eastbourne in the United Kingdom where she lives with her husband, two children and two cats. She is currently pursuing a degree in English Literature and Creative Writing and spends much of her time with her friend Mercedes Prunty who has helped publish this book. They are both Twenty-One Pilots fans and met through their love of music and writing.

Why not check out her socials and keep in touch...

Blog – www.pipernuelle.com
Instagram - @Pipernuelle
TikTok – @Piper.Nuelle
YouTube - @PiperNuelle

Death's Carousel

Death's Carousel
Copyright ©: Piper Nuelle and Mercedes Prunty
1st Edition: 2025
Publisher: Mercedes Prunty

The right of Piper Nuelle to be identified as author of this works and Mercedes Nicki Prunty as publisher has been asserted by them in accordance with sections 77 and 78 of the Copyright Act 1988. All rights reserved. This book is sold subject to the condition that it shall not, by way of trade or otherwise, be lent, hired out or otherwise circulated in any form of binding or cover other than that of which it is published. No part of this publication may be reproduced, stored in a retrieval system, copied in any form or by any means, electronic, mechanical, photocopying, recording or otherwise transmitted without written permission from the publisher. You must not circulate this book in any format.

This book is a work of fiction. Names, Characters, Incidents, Dialogues and Songs are the product of the authors imagination or are used fictitiously. Any resemblance to actual people living and or dead or events or songs is entirely coincidental.

ISBN – 978-1-0681848-1-9

Piper Nuelle

Death's Carousel

For my family, my best friend and for my sanity. I love to write and promise to myself to never stop writing again. But I thank my youngest daughter for making me listen to her music that re-ignited the idea that I just had to write down from a memory of an idea from years ago. And for my eldest daughter and my husband, for just being there and putting up with the same playlist for months and months on end.
Love you all xoxo

Another big thank you to Melanie Martinez, who's music woke up my dormant creative side and gave me the inspiration to write again. And to everyone who works alongside her musically. Music, writing and art all marry together as one
xo Piper xo

Trigger warning –
This book may have scenes and themes of an upsetting nature.

*Bullying
*Murder
*Self-harm suggestion
*Kidnap attempt
*Eating Disorder mention

Death's Carousel

Piper Nuelle

Chapter One... Death's Carousel...

Motion sickness, that feeling of nausea that ricochets through your entire body and can last for hours, so many hours and hours, even after you have got off the damn thing that is causing it, making your legs buckle, your stomach churn, your balance becomes non-existent, but it doesn't help when your spinning, spinning round and round, up and down, round and round, almost like the feeling of being drunk but not in a good fun way. No, this feeling is something else, it rides up from the pit of your being to spew out of your mouth like some gunge infested alien.

Up, down, round and round, up, down, round and round like a horse on a Merry-Go-Round. Spinning, churning, up and down, burning, spinning, turning, bile rising...

Nancy's eyes flew open, the bile having risen so far in her throat she was ready to throw up. She felt drunk, no, not drunk... drugged! She felt distant, not really in her body, like an out of body experience, but she was coming

Death's Carousel

back. Her eyes tried to grasp on to something to see where she was, but the spinning was altering her state of mind, her eyes couldn't focus, everything was a blur of greys, blacks and colourful, flashing, blinding lights.

Cheesy carnival music was playing in the background of the flying colours, and there was an almost off sweet scent in the air. A cross between cotton candy floss and decay. The smell, it made her stomach gurgle, it was like a sickly-sweet death. She could feel it on her tongue, taste the bittersweet granules of sugar that floated from a machine nearby, a machine that was rotten to its mechanical core.

The bile rose again, and she threw her hands up to her mouth, only, they didn't reach, a clunk of metal sounded out above the carnival beat. Vomit spewed from her mouth, it dribbled down her chin and over her jeans with a wet slap. She lowered her head down to where her hands could reach and she wiped the excess from her mouth, Then, she saw the glint of silver on her wrists… Handcuffs!

She instinctively shook her hands trying to loosen the cuffs on her, but they had been clasped to both wrists and wrapped around the faded gold of the pole that went straight through the plastic horse and to the floor of the huge mechanical ride. She looked around herself and the dizzying horse that held her hostage, the pole belonging to a real Carousel horse that was turning in a clockwise direction, the huge plastic animal rising up and down to the beat of the music. Reaching as far as she could feel, she could feel a saddle beneath her, the trainers she wore were also tied to the stirrups with cable ties, stopping both her arms and her legs from moving, stopping her from making any attempt to escape. *What the hell is going on?* Her mind raced.

Nancy tried to calm the panic that was rising feverishly within her, she tried to slow her breathing, she needed to take stock of where she really was and to see if anyone else was here with her. She tried to focus her eyes and decided that she was already feeling and being sick, so what was a little bit more motion sickness.

The horses that danced around her, bowing as they lowered down, and galloping as they rose back up, were all in some form of decayed state. The paint had peeled off them in large patches, revealing the base coat of the plastic horse beneath. It was eerie, the horses with peeled off eyes, peeled off nostrils and some with chunks taken right out of them. Some with missing hooves, some bald from the plastic hair having been ripped off, others had only the bottom pole holding them into place, they swayed wonkily in tune with the carousel music.

The central pillar of the Carousel had flashing lights dancing around a mirrored central unit, the mirrors smashed with sharp and jagged edges, and they reflected back a scared and worried face, her own. Nancy looked at herself in one of the shards, her eyes were red and puffy from throwing up and the drugged ill feeling, her mouth had crusted vomit in the corners, her mascara had run down her face like raccoon stripes, her bleach blond hair swayed in the air, with some parts plastered to her face by the sweat, tears and vomit that congealed like a glue to her skin. Her dark roots where she had a brown root smudge shone with a red glow as the flashing lights danced from colour to colour and flashing onto a crimson blood red tone, it looked like she was bleeding from her scalp. But in a flash of blue light, she went back to having brown roots again.

She shook herself mentally, *that was weird, must be tripping from being drunk or drugged*! She had to be, she never had thoughts of blood dripping from her skull. But… *something about this scene felt all too familiar, like Déjà vu, like she had witnessed something like this before!* Again, she shook her head, *how could she have seen this before? She had never been trapped or tied to a carousel horse before? To a bed maybe… But not… This!*

The unkempt and abandoned looking Carousel kept on spinning. Nancy spotted a control panel, it whipped past her in a flash, she saw that a lever had been tied in place with some rope, clearly to keep the Carousel going and never stopping. She craned her neck looking and thought, *If only there was something to throw at it, to dislodge it? Or to get someone to pull it? But then if someone else was here, maybe they were the one who put her here? Not to be trusted!*

Her blood ran cold, she hadn't even considered how she had even got here. *But, how? How had someone got her here, put her on this ride and cuffed her to it? Especially without her knowing, she would have kicked off about it… Must be the drugs, someone had to have drugged her and brought her here, but why? And was she alone? Or was anyone else here?* But she had no recollection, nothing, nada… No inkling of how or why she was here.

"Mhmmm", someone she couldn't see moaned, their voice, a murmur sounded from the other side of the

Carousel. Nancy's heart pounded, *was it friend or foe?* The voice had sounded groggy, like how Nancy had felt just a few moments ago. Either way she had to know.

"Hello? Anyone else here?" She called out.

Silence, or at least it was for a few seconds.

"Nancy? That you? It's me… Leanne!"

Nancy's heart skipped a beat, Leanne, a voice and person she knew, "Are you tied up too?" She called back out.

"Yeah", Leanne replied, "Where the hell are we?"

"No idea", Nancy said, "But my guess, the old, abandoned fairground down by Riverside?"

"Yeah, makes sense…But why?" Leanne asked.

Nancy shrugged then remembered they couldn't see one another, "Don't know… Is anyone else here?"

Another female voice mumbled from in front of her somewhere, "Mhmmm I'm here, and Mario too".

"Marielle?" Leanne exclaimed from her side of the carousel.

"Yup", she sounded just as groggy and as sick as Nancy felt.

"Is Mario, ok?" Nancy asked.

"He's still out", she replied, "You telling me you actually care about him Nance", Marielle then questioned her, in a kind of playful way, but also not.

Nancy sighed, Mario being Marielle's brother had made things difficult between them a little over the years, especially since he had the hots for her, but she didn't share those feelings for him, and Marielle being her best friend, well it was just awkward, especially since he would do anything for her if she asked… And she asked, a lot.

Death's Carousel

"I care that we are all here, on this… ride…" she trailed off as Leanne cut her off.

"Jared's here too, passed out in a carriage in front of my horse".

Nancy wondered why Jared was here. He was a kind of friend, mainly to Leanne and Tristan, Lee's Fiancé, but not really to Nancy and or Marielle. Although, it was looking like their friendship group was here, well, most of them. Luke and Sinead didn't seem to be present, unless they too were passed out in carriages that Nancy and the others couldn't quite see.

She tried to do another look about, twisting her head and straining her eyes, but it just made her feel queasy again. Her stomach churned, it felt like something was crawling through her insides. The vomit moving around inside her, waiting to make another appearance.

"What the actual hell is going on? Why are we on some stupid ride and chained up? This is some sick shit!" Leanne cried out from where she was chained. "And where is Tristan? If we are all here, then why isn't he?"

Nancy thought about Tristan, *could he have brought them here? As a weird, sick joke? To prank his soon to bride? But then Sinead and Luke not being here was also weird, they all came as a large team.* "Maybe he's being kept somewhere else? Sinead and Luke aren't here either".

"Weird… I don't like it", Marielle said, and they all agreed.

Suddenly the tempo of the carnival music changed, almost like a DJ changing a track… But this tempo change caused the Carousel to speed up too, as if the new version, 'remixed' the Carousel's mood, as if it had a mind of its own.

"Ha, Ha, very funny. You've had your fun… Now let us off", Nancy demanded trying to sound strong, even if inside she was a trembling mess.

But the Carousel continued to speed up, lights flashed faster, the images her eyes caught blurring into a smudge of nothingness. She tried to turn her head to see if she could see the person doing this to them, but the G-force of the ride made it hard to turn or move her neck, her head feeling heavy, like it weighed so much more than it should have. This felt wrong, so, so, wrong! *How could a carousel, a fun fair ride move in such a way? Surely it should be governed, restricted by some sort of fuse or sensor?*

"Hello? Are you listening to me? Stop this, NOW!" She cried out again, but her words were lost into the blur.

The speed was really picking up, she could feel the old machinery rattle, shake and rumble from the exertion on its metal innards. Carousels weren't built for speed, they were built for slow, joyous and carefree childlike fun, but this was sickening.

Her head spinning, her belly flopping, she just sat there and waited. There was nothing she could do other than just sit there and wait, wait for the person to stop it, or for it to fall apart and crash and burn to the decaying, cotton candy ground. She closed her eyes, her mind no longer able to cope with the spinning and blurring or the greying colours. She felt vomit rise in her throat again, the spinning turning her insides out.

Death's Carousel

Then darkness, a figure, or just a void, either way, darkness came for her...

*

A voice sounded out in the air, a sweet melodic voice, almost too sweet, sickly sweet, a sweetness that gets stuck in your teeth and you have to pick it out with your nails or dental floss.

Nancy's eyes fluttered open, she'd passed out again, her head resting on the cold golden pole of her Carousel horse. The coolness of the pole was actually comforting on her feverish skin, she was hot, too hot. She swallowed and felt something wriggle in her throat. She sat bolt upright, she coughed and tried to claw at her mouth, but her chained hands prevented her from reaching in.

"Ahh", she coughed harder trying to expel whatever was in her mouth.

A final cough and the thing flew out, it was a grub of some sort, like a large maggot.

"What the fuck", she whispered to herself. Then something came to her. As she was passing out a cloaked figure all in black came to her. It came from the central column, where the shattered mirrored glass distorted the world. It rammed something down her throat, it had tasted like rotting flesh and candy. Then it was gone as she passed out... But she remembered the things scent, its aroma, its smell... it smelled sweet, like a sweet berry perfume, it smelt familiar...

"No, no, no", she cry whispered, someone had put bugs inside her, they were crawling all over her insides, trying to get out. "Why?" ... A distant memory was trying to make its way through her mind, but her mind was clouded, fogged over by a cloud of rotten cotton candy floss... *But this all seemed like something that had happened before, in the past, at this very ride. What was it? Why couldn't she remember?*

    The voice sounded again, pulling Nancy away from her panicked and shocked state of mind, the sweet voice called out in the air and began to sing. The carnival music changed in tune with her voice.

    "Merry-Go-Round, Merry-Go-Round, on a Carousel, the dead go... Merry-Go-Round, Merry-Go-Round, on a Carousel, the dead know... Running away won't get you far, in this Nightmare, but you can try... Merry-Go-Round, Merry-Go-Round, On a Carousel... The dead show..." The girls voice sang out, her soft, sweet childlike voice carried in the sweet wind of the spinning air. The bulbs flashing in tune with each syllable. "Merry, Merry-Go-Round, Merry, Merry-Go-Round, Merry, Merry-Go-Round, Merry, Merry-Go-Round..."

    The sickness inside Nancy began to grow once again, the crawling bugs inside her mixing and burning in her stomach acid, some trying to crawl back up and out. The feeling nauseated her, the sweet taste of bile rising, making her mouth water. Her skin continued to burn, to flush with the fever and sickness in her body and her soul. The carousel jolted and sped up again, Nancy's stomach and mind turning to dizzying movements. She began to heave, feeling the putrid hotness as the wriggling and writhing wetness spewed from her mouth and all down her front. Her off-white blouse top she had paired with her jeans, her go to formal come casual look now was stained. It had become a new attire altogether with oranges, greys and red pustules of glob from melting insects and bug innards.

"Come ride the thestral, the horse of death, on this Carousel, don't lose your breath, come take deaths hand, so you'll understand, why you're here… At the Merry-Go-Round… Round… You Go".

The sweet melodic voice mixed bitterly with the sour toxic taste that now ravaged Nancy's mouth. *Water, she needed water…*

She felt her body rock side to side, she was trying to stay awake, but with each Carousel rotation she felt darkness trying to grasp at her, to make her pass out again. But she tried to fight it, passing out brought a new terror each time she awoke back up, so she needed to stay awake, to prevent the sweet demon from attacking her soul as she slept.

"And it's all fun and pain, this is deaths game… One of you will die and you won't make it off …The ride. So try, try to run and hide…"

The last note hit Nancy hard, square on in the chest, she tried, tried so hard to pull whatever strength she had left inside her to pull herself up.

"Did you hear that? Did you fucking hear that?" Leanne screamed from somewhere in the blur.

Nancy had almost forgotten the others were with her on this ride to hell, for some reason it felt personal to her and her alone.

"One of us is going to die on this ride! Like what the actual…"

Nancy blocked out Leanne's ramblings, Nancy knew it was herself that was going to die on this ride, no one else, not the others, only her. *The reason... the reason why...* was on the tip of her tongue but it wasn't quite there yet, it wasn't fully revealed... but it would be soon.

Tears streamed down Nancy's face as she trembled with fear, regret, and guilt as the songstress started a new verse.

"Merry-Go-Round, Merry-Go-Round, on a Carousel, the dead go, Merry-Go-Round, Merry-Go-Round, on a Carousel, the dead know... Running away won't get you far, in this Nightmare, but you can try..."

A flash of shards of mirror in the blinking, flashing fairground lights... A dark shadow...

"Are you too stupid and slow, how can you not know? What you... What you... did! To me...eeee..." A slight pause and then she continued on, "I'm not a freak, but how dared you speak, you tore my soul, but now your souls on show..."

Nancy tried desperately to listen deeply to the lyrics being sung to her and only her, she wanted and needed to understand why she was here, *why she was being punished, maybe why they were all here. Would finding the truth save her, save them?*

"Please, please just tell me why I'm here, what did I do wrong? What did we do so, so wrong?" She cried, hot tears rolled down her cheeks. She wanted to wipe away the hot stinging tears, but her cuffed wrists wouldn't reach. She screamed and thrashed around, pulling at the hand cuffs, desperately trying to loosen them up or to break the horse so she could break free. She tried kicking her feet, thrashing her legs about in the hopes something, anything would give.

"And it's all fun and pain, this is deaths game, one of you will DIE… And you won't make it off… The ride. So, try, try to run and hide!"

The word die was sung louder than the others, as if to reiterate how dangerous this unknown situation really was. This was definitely not a game. The girls sweet, angelic voice carried around the whole Carousel bouncing off the lights and the chipped, smashed broken sharded, mirror. Just like the bugs that bounced off her with every bump in the rotation of the old, decrepit fairground ride.

She shook her head, she had to be hallucinating, words didn't bounce. *And maybe there weren't really any bugs? Maybe it was all in her head? Surely her stomach acid would have boiled them all alive… Surely, they couldn't still be writhing and moving inside her.* She pulled again harder at the cuffs, blood began to drip down as they cut into her skin, but she felt no pain, she pulled harder, strips of her flesh began to peel off, almost like the decaying carousel horses, whose plastic flesh had peeled off over time.

"Merry-Go-Round, Merry-Go-Round, on a Carousel, the dead go, Merry-Go-Round, Merry-Go-Round, on a Carousel, the dead know… Running away won't get you far, in this Nightmare, but you can try, Merry-Go-Round, Merry-Go-Round, On a Carousel… The dead show."

The voice seemed to be getting closer, Nancy glanced around to see if a speaker was close to her, or falling on her… A shadow… A Flash of a face… Another

Shadow... A microphone. "Why did you hate me? And you had no heart? You had no reason, to make the chaos start! My life was ruined, and torn apart, but now I've grown and I'm powerful, so now... It's your turn, your turn... YOUR TURN... To die or at least try..." She then lowered her voice to a mere whisper, "Not too..."

The last note was carried by her voice, her tone turning from melodic sweetness to a more bitter note, menacing and evil.

Pure fear spread through Nancy's body, she could feel it, the song would end soon and with it, her life. Unless she did something now. She pulled at the cuffs harder than before. Skin splitting, muscle bursting through... "Must get out, it will hurt now... But I'll be alive... Must be alive...Need to get out...Now". She spoke only to herself through gritted teeth as she pulled, dark blobs and sparkles from stars flashed in her peripheral vision. Pain rippled through her as she twisted, pulled, yanked, kicked, screamed, SNAP!

"Ahh, Ahh... Ahh", she cried out in horrific pain as her bone snapped tearing and bursting through her flesh, but the wrong way, it had snapped behind the cuff, meaning as she pulled the metal bracelet it caught on the bone and wouldn't go over her hand. The pain was so unreal, intense, and she couldn't muster up the strength to pull it over the protruding bone. Blood blossomed down her palms and over the horse's face, giving it an evil, blood thirsty demeanour.

She leant forward trying to cradle her wrist, but the cuffs and the rotation of the machine made it hard to do. Movement at the mirrored column caught her attention and

Death's Carousel

she sobbed as a face she recognised came into view and sang… "Merry-Go-Round, Merry-Go-Round, On a Carousel… The dead go…"

"Please I'm so sorry, I remember, I remember what I did to you and I'm so, so, sorry".

"Merry-Go-Round, Merry-Go-Round, On a Carousel… The dead know…"

"Please" … She whispered.

"Running away won't get you far, In this Nightmare, But you can try…"

The threat felt so deep and personal as those dark, deep, piercing eyes looking into Nancy's, literally piercing her soul… She had heard the threat before, of trying to run but not getting very far before… Because it had come from Nancy's own mouth… Many years ago…

*   *   *

Nancy smiled as she took in the sweet smell of success and friendship that came from the cotton candy carnival air that surrounded her. Screams of joy sounded out around her at the Riverside Fun Fair. Children, Teenagers and Adults alike all enjoying themselves on the rides with the flashing lights that pulled and twisted their stomachs till they wanted to puke. Cheesy carnival music thumped around them, the joyous screams almost a part of the music being played.

Sweets, hotdogs, cotton candy floss, popcorn, burgers, chips, fizzy pop and all things unhealthy being consumed by the masses of people looking for a quick sugar high. Teenagers smuggling in bottles of vodka and getting drunk by the huge Ferris wheel that hung over the fun fair like an illuminated beacon of chaos and fun times. Smoke from their illegal cigarettes, weed and the new thing, vapes, creating a sickly fog of sweetness and tobacco.

Nancy stood waiting, she was meant to be meeting Leanne and one other girl… A girl they had decided to prank today on one of rides.

Nancy hadn't considered herself a bad person, her mum and dad always told her that she was a good girl… but that she could be easily led. That sounded good to her, why would she want to take responsibility for her own actions when she could pass the buck onto someone else. Especially Leanne, everyone knew she was the ringleader, the top bitch and head 'Mean Girl', at school and no one, not even her parents liked to upset her and have her wrath thrown at them. *'She could get away with murder that one'*, she had heard people say on many occasions.

Nancy once would have said she herself was a kind girl, but kindness got her nowhere. Kindness had made her friends with the weird, freaky girl at school, a girl whose friendship had got Nancy picked on, again, on many occasions. But now Nancy was a teenager, in her prime, her peak. She had great boobs, nice hair, straight teeth, and her parents had good jobs and money. So, *why should she keep getting bullied because of her 'poor', 'ugly', 'freaky' friend.* The friend who had no money, her parents were alcoholics and had abandoned her, her nan, her guardian, clothed her in hand me downs, her hair was greasy and matted, her teeth wonky, her skin pimply and she had a flat chest to boot. Nancy was becoming a social butterfly, she

Death's Carousel

wanted to spread her wings and fly the nest. Meet new people, get a boyfriend…maybe… or… get the person she wanted and desired the most… maybe… get invited to the hottest parties in town. And her friend…well, maybe… the freaky friend… Just wasn't great for her image anymore. Yeah, she was a nice girl, she had been there for Nancy when her parents nearly split, her dad had been gambling and gambled most of the house away, only by a stroke of luck did they get to keep it, a company bought their house from them and then rented it back to them, that way no one had to know, in all honesty, people still thought they owned it… And when she had fallen and chipped her tooth, freaky girl, she'd held her hand at the dentist when they fixed it… calmed her racing mind of the panic that she had ruined her teeth, ruined her good looks and ruined any chance of becoming, 'cool'. But she had outgrown her now. Plus, now she was in with Leanne and her group, that meant Leanne demanded a certain amount of 'Pranks' to be dished out to the 'UGLIES' and today was one such day, a day to prank an 'Ugly', and the ugly in question just happened to be Nancy's old friend.

Feeling the warmth of the sun's rays that beat down upon her as she waited for them to arrive. Of course, Leanne arrived first, they had told the 'Ugly' to arrive a bit later so they could implement their plan of action. Leanne's perfect celebrity smile peered out from her already lip filled lips, at only fourteen, Leanne had already had filler and Botox, her mum was aesthetically trained in that field and let her daughter do what she wanted to her face and body.

Pink gloss glittered over her plumped pout and sparkled in the sun, along with her grey blue eyes and caramel blond hair. Leanne was slim, had the perfect body type too, big *'Kardashian'* bum, big boobs, slim legs and toned abdomen. She worked out in her home gym daily and lived on hummus and celery to maintain her healthy figure.

Nancy felt ugly next to Leanne, but then so did most of the girls in their year group, the school as a whole and well, most of the town, even the female teachers envied her body and fitness routine.

"You ready?" She asked licking her lips with anticipation.

Nancy nodded, "Yeah, I got the things". She lifted a bag and handed it to Leanne,

Leanne took the bag and rummaged through, she pulled out a set of handcuffs, fluffy ones that were meant for the bedroom but would work just as well for what they needed, she was sure her parents wouldn't miss those for a while. And a round foil, encasing a soiled and putrid lunch ready for their 'ugly' to consume.

"What's in it?" Leanne asked, her bright eyes shining with glee.

"A…er… mouldy cheeseburger", Nancy replied with a grin.

Leanne nodded her head in approval, "Now all we need are some bugs to accompany it". They walked around the fair looking for broken ground where worms and other bugs may be lurking. It didn't take them long, a patch of soil with worms where birds had been pecking for their dinner, but it was also by a bin, where things had rotten away in the hot summer heat, perfect bug weather. Leanne laughed with joy at the sight of some maggots wiggling around, "These are perfect", she lifted the foil and opened the rancid burger bun and scooped the maggots and worms up and placed them in the burger. Ready for consumption. "A little bit of extra protein won't hurt her, ha".

The pair of snickering teenagers wondered on over to the Bumper car ride, that was the meeting point to meet, 'The Ugly' of the day. A few minutes passed and a shy, sweet, melodic voice called out to Nancy,
"Hi…Um…Nancy, I'm here".

The voice belonged to Kayella, she was a thin, ghostly looking girl with dark piercing eyes that should have been full of life and confidence, but instead they sparkled with a painful shyness. Long dark lashes fluttered as she looked down at her feet, she held one hand in another. Her long dark raven blue-black hair hung limply down her back, it lacked lustre and desperately needed a cut. Braces lined her teeth and as she spoke, she tried to hide her teeth in an awkward way that made them more obvious. Her clothes, a size or two too big for her, clearly hand me downs from her chubby cousin in the year above who other than passing down clothes had absolutely nothing to do with her. She wore a black T-shirt with a bands name and logo on, the size of the T made her look even smaller chested than she already was, her jeans were baggy at the knees from overwearing, and the bottoms were too long and trailed on the floor, snags at the hem were torn and raggedy.

Nancy looked at Kayella and sighed, *it was a shame, Kayella was a nice girl, her life had just been a bit 'shit'*. Nancy remembered the day she first spoke to Kayella at the park. She had been playing on some swings by herself, the other kids are ignoring her, but Nancy had said hi, and that's where their friendship began. Nancy's mum had invited Kayella around for dinner and it became an almost weekly occurrence, she became like part of their family. Her mum stating, 'I feel sorry for the girl, at least here she gets one hot meal a week'.

Kayella's parents were... not to be desired. Her dad, an alcoholic had left her as a baby, he had wanted a boy and was disgusted he had been blessed with a girl. He moved away and started a family with someone else, also became clean and pledged to never drink a drop of alcohol ever again. Kayella had been most upset when it turned out she had a half-sister, not a brother or boy in sight, but the dad had stayed and looked after the girl and the mother, worshipped the ground they walked on. Her mother... became ill when Kayella was five, died soon after, liver disease from all the booze she consumed. She ended up having to live with her nan, who whilst lovely, had dementia and whittled away her money betting on horses and smoking. Most nights she forgot she was looking after a child and made no meal or had no food in the house, but there was always a bottle of whisky on the side, her *'night, night'* medicine she called it.

Nancy for a brief moment felt pure guilt ripple through her body, it wasn't Kayella's fault at the life she had, it wasn't her fault she was poor, had no money... but Nancy just wanted to fit in. She was fed up with being friends with the freak and getting bullied herself for it. The bullying was in no way comparable to what the bullies used against Kayella, but it still wasn't fun. And like she thought before, *she wanted a boyfriend, she was glowing up,*

Death's Carousel

becoming prettier, and more noticed… But Kayella held her back from her true potential.

"Kayella darling, so nice you could make it", Leanne smirked taking her arm and leading her towards the carousel, "We have a treat for you today!"

"I … Ur… didn't mean to intrude on your day", Poor Kayella tried to turn away, wiggling her arm to try and get Leanne to release her grip on it. But the movement made Leanne grip hold tighter.

"Intrude? You're the entertainment for our day… Darling", Leanne laughed, the word 'Darling', a purr, an irritating purr that made Nancy's shit itch, but it was better having Leanne on side than not, and for that she could ignore the word she used to sound posh and above people. Leanne began to lead Kayella through the throng of people that were queuing up for the Bumper car ride.

They walked through the crowd and made their way through to the Carousel, their chosen spot for that day's prank. As they approached, the warmth of the sun's rays began to fade as a cloud took refuge above the lights of the flashing ride. The shadow cast an eerie vibe to emit from the faces of the plastic horses, their eyes dancing a glowing red from the lights that danced above them. The gloom from the light show gave the horses a grimy, slimy look about them. And what made it eerier was the fact that no one else was queuing up for the ride, it was as if the ride was holding its breath and waiting for them to climb on, waiting just for Kayella.

Nancy led Kayella onto the ride and took her to a lone horse that sat at the back of the ride where no eyes could see them due to the central column blocking the way.

Leanne stalked off to the ride operator. Nancy watched as Leanne arranged her top to show off more cleavage, the young boy operator who was no more than nineteen blushed beetroot red as she whispered sweet nothings into his ear. He nodded something in agreement. Nancy smiled, that meant he was game, and it meant they could execute their fun plan.

Kayella sat on the horse, her face gaunt looking from the knowing sadness that something horrible was about to happen. Her hair hid her face like a curtain and her hands…. well Nancy took the cuffs out from her bag and noticed how calm Kayella was and didn't even protest about her hands being cuffed to the fairground ride.

Leanne scurried over, a look of pure evil glee in her eyes, "Well the guys in, said he will keep the ride going till I say so. Unless his Uncle comes back then he will have to stop the ride, but he's at another ride so…" Leanne studied Kayella, her eyes flickering with annoyance, "Um… Your meant to be whinging and trying to escape".

Kayella didn't respond.

"She didn't even flinch when I put the cuffs on, it's almost like she doesn't care anymore", Nancy scoffed.

A cruel smirk spread across Leanne's lips, "Well…She will care in a second", and she leant over to Nancy's bag. Nancy looked, her eyes catching a glimpse of Leanne's cleavage, an intrigued feeling crossed her mind as Leanne's skin glowed from the body makeup she had used to try and enhance her assets for the ploy of getting the boy involved. The shimmer made them look soft, smooth and… Kayella's hair shifted, and she made eye contact with Nancy, a knowing look filtered into her eyes. Nancy felt

Death's Carousel

heat rise in her cheeks, embarrassed that she had been caught looking at Leanne in that way. Nancy stiffened up, pure anger and rage bubbling in her blood, how dare she look at her in that questioning way! Nancy wasn't a lesbian, she just couldn't help but look… They were, just there… She hated it, hated that Kayella had caught her out. Kayella had asked Nancy once if she was gay, but Nancy came from a respected Christian household, her parents would never allow it! So, she denied it. But Kayella knew, she always knew things… her cool dark eyes shining with an almost second sight.

Nancy snatched the rotting food from Leanne's hand. Leanne looking shocked then happy at her eagerness to exact torture on the freaky girl.

Nancy grabbed Kayella's hair and pulled causing her to wince in pain, her mouth opening ever so slightly as she cried out, but it was enough. She opened her mouth just enough for Nancy to ram the rotting burger into her mouth. Kayella thrashed around trying desperately to get away from her grasp and the wriggling, writhing food that Nancy was forcing further and further down her throat, pure anger making her choke and gag the girl she had once been friends with.

Leanne cackled with glee at the sight and took out her phone and began taking photos and videos, cheering on her friend. Kayella's hair whipped from side to side as she pulled her head away. She spat out the disgusting food, worms and maggots glistened with wetness from her saliva having touched them. The girls laughed, Leanne filming the whole event now. Filming as Nancy cried with laughter as she punched and kicked the freak on the horse she couldn't escape from.

Eventually the girls backed off the ride and gave a signal, the Carousel started up, its gears whirring into action, the cheesy music blasted out from the speakers, the lights flashed and danced all around Kayella. She sat sobbing, hot streams of tears fell down her porcelain cheeks, like a China doll ready to give up and break.

The ride turned, the plastic colourful horses lifting up and falling back down in time with the carnival music. A stale breeze of cotton candy floss and decaying meat washed over Kayella, as did a wave of nausea. Bile rose in her throat along with her horse that rose up, lights beamed in her eyes, her tears making colourful streams beam all around her like an aura. The feeling of the maggots on her tongue made her stomach heave. The horse she rode waivered in her rainbow light, distorting, changing shape, its paint peeling off revealing a skeleton horse beneath. The putrid meet and bugs poisoned her, the sickness from the motion of the ride causing an hallucination, panic, an anxiety attack.

More tears, floods of tears but they were useless as no one would come to her aid, because no one ever did.

A bell chimed to signal the end of the ride, but it wasn't the end for Kayella. Leanne looked at the boy, pouted her lips and squeezed her bust to make her breasts pop. He smiled an awkward yet hungry smile and pulled the lever to start the ride again. The cheesy music pounding down upon Kayella. The screams of other fun fair users drowned out her own as she cried to be let off.

Death's Carousel

The screams and laughter of Leanne and Nancy echoed through her soul, tears streaming down her face like a baby. Both Nancy and Leanne made crying motions with their hands, "Boo Hoo… Look at the little baby crying for her mummy… Ha Ha Ha…"

The hot bile rising in her throat again, her crying making the heaving worse. Then with a wave of hot liquid, vomit spewed out all down her. Her hands being cuffed meant she couldn't move to not aim it at herself. The hot putrid wetness clung to her clothes, spotted in her hair and dripped down her chin. She felt humiliated!

A crowd of other kids from their school had arrived, Leanne's videos had gone viral throughout the school network, alerting all the fun fair teens to her hell ride. None of them wanted to ride the ride, but to watch, to stare, to gloat and to film.

Laughter filled the sweet air, tears of overindulgent glee drowned out the dizzying sobs from the freaky girl. Spinning, crying, laughing, lights flashing, music booming, tears, fears… She wanted a big black hole to swallow her up, she wanted everyone to disappear…She…

"Let her off", a male voice sounded out over the sound of the cheesy music.

The boy in charge of the Carousel looked ashamed as another boy approached him and demanded he stop the ride. The lever was pulled, and the Carousel began to slow down, but it was too late, the humiliation was too much, everyone had seen it, and those who hadn't soon would via videos on social media.

The crowd of kids booed as the ride slowed to a halt, then a cheer as the ride stopped with her at the front in full view of everyone. The boy who stopped the ride came over and tried to tackle the hand cuffs, but they didn't budge. Looking around he demanded the keys, but of course non were given up.

In all the commotion a man came running over to the ride and saw what had happened, the cuffs, the rotting food, the girl trapped. It must have been the uncle of the ride operator, he screamed abuse at the boy, smacking him round the ear and demanded he get a tool from his workshop near the Dodgems. Within minutes the man had bolt cutters and had cut the cuffs off her wrists and Kayella was free… Free to be devoured by the crowd.

But the boy… the boy stayed with her. Told everyone to do one. He helped clean her up, got her a bottle of water, made her feel… calm.

Nancy on the other hand was furious. Leanne's video had been sent out on social media, it had gone viral around the school and a teacher had informed her mum of the incident. It only incriminated Nancy, it showed her beating the freak, feeding the freak, cuffing her and laughing at her. Her Christian parents so ashamed of their daughter besieged by the Devil himself. She was grounded for months and forced to write an apology letter to Kayella.

'Sorry, not sorry for what I did. You were going to rat me out to my secret love that I hid, sorry, not sorry I don't want no peace, there will be no olive branch from this mouthpiece.

Sorry, not sorry for what I said, test me again and you will be dead. Sorry, not sorry, that your

Death's Carousel

done in the head, being friends with you gave me no street cred.

The Carousel torture was just a start, because you saw into my true heart. I will get revenge for me being grounded, I will make sure that your head will be pounded.

Running away won't get you far... but you can try, you can try, you can try, try, try!'

Nancy xoxo

*　　　　*　　　　*

Nancy came back to the present in a flood of guilt, shame, nausea and pain. She could hear the 'so called', apology letter sung to her in her mind, as if the song on the Carousel had paused... But she could hear it, her threat, the very threat that Kayella now used in some form of Karmic payback.

She peered into the eyes of the girl's life she had been friends with and then betrayed, because of some stupid crush she'd had on a girl. She'd made out to herself and others that it was because she just wanted a boyfriend, for a guy to notice her... But she had denied her true self and her true feelings to come to light, she had hidden them, swept them under the carpet. But Kayella, she had seen the truth, she had known the truth, and yet she never judged her, she had still wanted to be Nancy's friend.

Kayella came into view, she looked different, but Nancy could see it was her. She'd definitely had a *'glow up'* since leaving school. Her face had more colour, she no longer looked like death warmed up. She wore makeup that looked to be professionally done, a smudged out smoky eye that accentuated her dark piercing, playful eyes. Her long lashes curled and filled in with more to frame her almond eye shape. Her lips, she'd had filler and had lined and glossed them with a beautiful shimmer gloss. Her hair was still the Raven blue darkness of the night, but it fell down in curled loose waves that framed her now curvy frame. She clearly worked out, a lot! And had boob implants done... Nancy remembered the shit they had given the poor girl over her flat chest, yet now she had the best boobs out of them all. She smelled sweet, soft, berry-like and yet elegant, a clean yet florally, berry sweet aroma. Nancy breathed her in, she had been so stupid to not want to be her friend.

    Nancy looked deep into those dark familiar eyes, once upon a time those eyes had loved her, supported her, but Kayella was different, something murderous twinkled behind them. They looked amused, as if she was laughing inside at a personal joke that only she knew.

    Nancy realised now that she had fallen for the wrong girl, Leanne had given her nothing but shit and used her because of the love she held inside for her, giving her a slight promise, a slight inclination that maybe one day... Things could be how Nancy desired them to be. But Kayella had loved Nancy as a friend... Nancy should have loved her back.

    "Kayella? I... I'm so sorry what we did to you... Please... I'm so, so, sorry", Nancy's lips trembled as the words came tumbling out. She could see Kayella cared not for how she felt and how sorry she was.

Kayella leant forward and breathed the last line of the song into her face, her sweet cherry scented breath washing over Nancy, "Merry-Go-Round, Merry-Go-Round… On death's Carousel… The dead show…"

The last line vibrated through Nancy's soul. She could see the threat, feel the violence now radiating from the girl's aura, from her very being. "Please…" She whispered, knowing full well all was lost. She shook the cuffs in a final defeated attempt to try and escape but everything, all life and strength faded from her body… She had given in.

The last musical melody caused the lights to dance in a way that looked like teeth coming for her. She wanted to cry out and scream, but nothing crossed her lips.

Kayella lifted her microphone and clicked a button upon it…

CLANK… CLANK… CLANK…

A mechanical vibration sounded out above Nancy's head, she glanced up to see a panel of the carousel rise up, in its place a large golden spike appeared, it had once been one of the horse's poles to keep one of them attached to the ride, but now it had been carved and sharpened to a deadly point.

Nancy let out a final scream of terror as Kayella pushed yet another button and the spike was thrust downwards towards her… It's victim.

A wet plunging noise splatted out from where Nancy sat. The spike had travelled down her throat and gullet and had penetrated through her spinal cord killing the girl instantly. Warm syrup-like blood began to pool out from the wound and dripped wetly and loudly down onto the metal platform of the fair ground ride in the now silence that filled the coming night air.

Screams echoed in unison, both Leanne and Marielle had heard the commotion of the spike falling and with Nancy's now lack of voice they knew something bad had happened.

Kayella stood in pure amusement at the fate that had befallen her once friend. She'd felt the warm splatters of blood flick up at her when the spike had fallen and pierced the girl from the inside out. A sense of accomplishment filled her veins, a warm fuzzy feeling that made her feel giddy with joy.

For years these people had terrorised her life, made her feel ugly inside and out. Made her feel that she had to change herself inside and out to finally fit in, to finally be accepted... *But now she was the powerful one, she was in control, and they would feel and witness her wrath.*

She spun on her heel and walked off the ride, she pulled up her cloak around her and pulled the hood over her hair and face. Yes, Nancy had seen who she was, but her plan had been to reveal herself to each one of them at the right moment, just before their passing, so they could feel the upmost terror. The others she wanted them to fear who she was, to fight amongst one another, argue about who they thought could be their killer. She wanted the cloak to scare them, to send chills down their spines as if she was the Grim Reaper! She hurried off, ducking down by a building that led to a play zone. Eventually they would

Death's Carousel

come looking, and she wanted to be ready for their own individual performances. It was all starting to feel bittersweet.

Chapter Two...Bouncy Razor Castle...

Sinead Wilson sat bolt upright, a piercing scream echoed through the dank darkness that surrounded her. The scream had sounded like someone was being murdered and it sent a sudden chill down her spine.

As she thought about the scream, she felt the bed she was on wobble beneath her. She couldn't see much in the gloom, so she sent her hands out to feel around her, but the bed seemed to go on forever around her. And the feel of it, a cold, plastic come rubbery texture. She quickly realised that she wasn't on a bed at all, not a waterbed or air bed, but the floor was moving, the floor was bouncy and rubbery... *A bouncy castle?*

"Where am I?" She whispered to herself in the darkness. She tried to recall her memories, tried to think where she was, or how she got there, but nothing entered her mind. The last thing she could remember was... *Leanne? Marielle? Maybe? Yes, she had been with them, Leanne had thrown a party, a huge house party and many were invited... A large cocktail bowl had been set out on*

Death's Carousel

the breakfast bar in the kitchen… They all drank, drank a lot… they danced… felt tired and then… Here!

"Leanne? Marielle? You here? What is this a joke?", She called out, but only the beat of her heart answered. She swallowed nervously, her mouth suddenly feeling dry, she needed a drink. Feeling around again she thought maybe she was in the garage… *Maybe for some reason Leanne had hired a bouncy castle? Although she couldn't think of why, Leanne and Tristan had no kids yet, and neither did any of them in their friendship group…*

She was cold and she shivered in the strange plastic arena. The smell of stale decayed food, sweat and plastic gripped her throat, making her mouth feel dryer than before. The dryness tickled her throat, and she coughed loudly into the air and as she did it set off something mechanical sounding.

Chhhhh, Chhhhh, Chhhhh…

Someone had flicked a switch to the lights, and they flicked on with a loud mechanical clicking noise. The sudden brightness disorientated Sinead and she tilted her head away from them, placing one hand over her face to shield her eyes. When the distortion faded, and her vision came back she gawped. Her mouth fell open in disbelief. She was in a children's play zone somewhere, it looked and felt familiar, but her fuzzy brain couldn't recall where from. She was indeed upon a bouncy castle, a large castle that was mouldy, had stains of some vile substance and had a thick layer of dust and grime settled over it. Clearly it had not been used for a really long time. She turned her head to look around the rest of the play zone area.

A small cafeteria style eatery sat to one side of the room, a serving hatch was closed with a condiment basket full of moulded sachets of sauces on the small shelf that sat with it. A few plastic tables and chairs were scattered around the area of the small cafeteria, some still standing, others had been trashed, splintered and spread all over the floor. Behind the food area was a large, netted area that had once been colourful but was now a muted expanse of peeling plastic balls, soft pads and terrifying animal shapes.

She went to move, a bad eerie feeling filled her with dread. *Why was she here? And where was Leanne and the others? Was this a prank? Or had someone taken her?*

The floor wobbled beneath her as she tried to stand, she put her hand on the grimy plastic wall to steady herself and shrieked in pain as something sliced into the palm of her hand. Reeling she pulled her hand close and inspected it. A thin line of blood trickled down her hand and onto the rubber floor. She looked at the wall and spotted a razor blade that had been crudely glued to it, her blood shining wetly on the rusted sliver of silver.

"What the fuck?" She whispered. She knew now something was more wrong than she had anticipated. She kept herself quiet as she looked around again. The lights danced around her as other flashes of rusted silver protruded from other parts of the castle. Someone had stuck these on intentionally to cause harm.

She bit her lip as the realisation hit her, *someone had kidnapped her!*

Weirdly she smiled, *she had her very first stan!* She was of course now a little bit of a celebrity, her friends called her a minor celeb, a 'Z' lister, but now she guessed

Death's Carousel

she had been promoted to major celeb status if she had a crazed person wanting to kidnap her. *Ha… Joke was on them…* She did have over 250,000 followers on social media and a growing modelling career to boot. She posted glamorous images daily to her fans, clothing hauls, designer brand deals, handbags, shoes, makeup and of course the brand paid holidays… Some of which she lied about, she just faked the photos for the grid, but people lapped them up like a cat to cream. *Fuck yeah, she had made it!* She was officially proper famous if some nut job had stolen her off the street. The glee quickly disappeared, and she fully understood the danger of the situation. If some crazy person had kidnapped her, then they could hurt her, and not just with razor blades glued to bouncy and rubbery walls. She needed to get out!

The good thing about Sinead was, she didn't scare easily, and she was resourceful. She didn't get to where she was without stepping on others toes with sharp, piercing nine-inch-high heels. She was ruthless, cutthroat and would do anything to succeed. This made her smile inside, a sense of being filled her body and she stood up again. She would get out, she would find the asshole and she would murder them for doing this to her and make out it was self-defence all along.

Treading carefully, she made her way along the bouncy walkway, she wobbled from side to side, her arms going out to steady herself, and she desperately tried to not nip herself on anymore of the razors, especially seen as some of them were rusted and she didn't fancy having a huge tetanus jab, although maybe she should seen as the first razor looked rusty red mixed with her blood. The walk was not an easy one, she chuckled to herself as she thought how she was used to catwalks and runway shows, definitely not wobbly fun house shit.

She made it to one end of the castle but found it to be a dead end, a random blown-up obstacle had been placed in the way, and it was littered with sharp objects to stop her from pushing it out the way or passing round it. She looked around, she could go back the way she came but she hadn't seen another way out... then she spotted on the outside of the castle a door and it had one of the green exit lights lit up above it, and it was just ahead of the spiked obstacle and through a kids play netted tunnel.

Her eyes darted back and forth trying to find another way, but nothing came to mind, and she couldn't be bothered to go back and try something else, that just seemed futile and a waste of her time.

She placed one hand on the spiked obstacle and grinned, "Just hot air, right?" To the left of her hand was a razor that hadn't been glued on properly and with a quick yank she had it in the palm of her hand.

Feeling triumphant inwardly she rammed the blade into the bouncy rubber, a thin slice appeared and then... POP-BANG...

The pressure of the bouncy castle obstacle being slit open caused it to explode outwards, the shards of sharps whizzing and slashing at Sinead. She ducked and rolled her body, trying to get out of the way of the blast but it had taken her completely by surprise. The noise of the blast made her hearing falter for a moment, and she thought she heard music begin to play but she also heard ringing tinnitus in her ears from the loud explosion.

Death's Carousel

She shook herself and felt stabs of pain in her abdomen, arms and cheeks. Her hand went up to her face first in blind panic, "Not my face, not my face", she whined. It wasn't due to vainness that she checked or at least that's what she told herself, but her face and her body were her career. If she became scarred, she would lose contracts and be turned away, she could lose her following and become a nobody again. She was NEVER going to be a nobody again, she had worked too hard to get to where she was, and the only way on her ladder to success was up, she would never climb back down the rungs to failure. Plus, she needed the attention, she craved the attention, she needed the validation from others to feel like she was at her best, like she had succeeded.

She examined her hand to see blood, one of the razors had sliced her cheek, but she had no mirror and no way to see the extent of the damage. She checked her arms and saw slice marks and scratches, luckily not deep but enough to draw blood and sting. But her stomach, she peered down at her revealing cream silk strappy designer top, a pool of blood had stuck the top to her tummy where a glittering shard of silver stuck out. A razor blade had embedded itself into her flesh, her blood was pooling out, sticking the top to her skin and turning it a washed out pink.

She winced in pain as she gently touched it, she couldn't remember if it was best to leave it in or pull it out? She tried to move, to stand with it still in, but a new searing sharpness rocked her body, the movement causing it to slice in deeper. Feeling a lack of hope of anyone finding her or coming to look for her before she bled out, she decided it needed to come out.

As she sat there gently clawing at the offending object the music she had heard began to play again, but this time louder and then a melodic sweet almost angelic voice joined in, a voice that sounded faintly familiar.

"Bouncy Razor Castle... Bouncy Razor Castle...

Why did I get an invite here? Now my blood is all over the party bags... Tell me why that everyone is here? Is it so they can poke and sneer, at me now?"

Sinead listened to the lyrics and felt confused, *a bouncy razor party? Like what the actual hell? Who does that?*

"Maybe this is a prank for me, again now, again now... Maybe the name Skank for me, is not the worst now... The worst now..."

Sinead looked down at the razor blade inside her, gritted her teeth and yanked it in one quick motion. She cried out in pain and felt the warmth of fresh blood pour down her stomach. Stars danced in front of her eyes, and she lay down on the cool plastic until the wave of dizziness passed.

She then pushed herself up. She didn't like this, not one bit, she had such a bad feeling that was welling up inside her, a raw panic. She looked down at her wound that was still pouring with the vibrant red liquid. She needed something to wrap around it, so stem the bleeding, to make it clot, but all she wore was her cream now pink stained strappy top and diamante embellished jeans and strappy wedge shoes, and she didn't want to walk around pretty much in the nude for some psycho weirdo stan to stare and leer at her.

"It's a castle, a bouncy razor castle, and I'll bleed if you make me, bleed, bleed, bleed… Let's bring out the cake and blow the candles out, I need help and I'm shouting out with doubt".

"Are you serious?" Sinead laughed with anger, she looked around the room, trying to find a camera or something watching her, she knew someone had to be. "Where are you? You sick fuck!"

No one replied back, only the soft rift of the melody.

Another verse began to play, and Sinead decided she needed to explore past the exploded obstacle, she needed out. She hauled herself up, a lightheaded feeling causing her head to spin.

She started up the wobbly passage, the remains of the obstacle creating a new problem of trying to make it across without stepping or falling onto the remaining sharp objects.

Hisssssssssssssss… A noise, like a thousand snakes ready to sink their fangs into flesh sounded out. Adding to her predicament was the realisation that the sharps had punctured the bouncy castle, and it was now deflating around her. The part she walked on became flatter and more awkward to walk steadily on, especially as vertigo fuelled her body, making her sway from side to side, a dizziness creeping in.

Her heart pounded in her chest as she desperately tried to make it over, her dizziness making it harder as the floor shifted underfoot, the hissing of air disorientating her.

She let out a sigh of relief as she made it across, but the relief didn't last for long, before her was a netted hole that the castle had been attached to and it led into a kid's soft play area, leading to the door with the exit sign, but she could hear a distant buzzing sound, not too dissimilar to the mad hissing but this was more of a hum, not a hiss, like an electrical current. She leant forward and examined the netted tunnel, and sure enough someone had set up car batteries with wires attached to the nets. Sinead peered in closer, as a kid she remembered the netted sections of kids play areas being just a skinny rope or a thick string, *surely it shouldn't be a conductor for an electrical current?* But as she looked, she saw someone had taken the time to wrap a metal wire around each rope section and then had clamped the wires from the batteries to them.

"Shit", she hissed in frustration, her voice echoing in the air around her.

There was no other way out, the bouncy castle itself was a sealed in unit with a roof and it was quickly deflating and vanishing around her, so she couldn't climb out, and she didn't want to end up trapped underneath a pile of heavy stinking plastic and rubber. She also couldn't risk cutting the net and being electrocuted or even walking over the net. And popping the castle was too dangerous after her previous experience, although she considered maybe it wouldn't pop like before as it was shrinking already, the pressure had already been released like a Kraken, but she wasn't sure she could hold up and cut the heavy duty rubber with a small sharp razor and make a hole big enough without passing out from exertion and lying in the pit of blades.

Death's Carousel

On closer inspection she noticed that the wires hadn't been wrapped around the whole tunnel, just the bottom, the walkway... If she could hold her own body weight she could hang and climb across the top and then lower herself down the other side, missing the electrical currents completely.

She took of her shoes and threw them over the other side, she wanted them back on when she reached the other side so as not to slice her feet on hidden razor blades that she anticipated to be waiting for her in the ball pit. God knows what other horrors awaited her that side from her creepy kidnapping stan. Then she grasped the net above her head with her hands and swung her legs and feet up to grip the netting with her feet and toes. She cried out, her wound pulling and ripping as she swung. She moved her legs first gripping the next row of net, her toes curling the rope as she tried to fit her feet in the small, netted holes. The stringy, ropey texture tore into her feet, and she had to try with all her might not to drop down. Next, she moved her arms and scrunched in a little to then move her feet out for the next section. She repeated this motion over and over until she was nearly across the void of instant death. She could feel her blood running down in rivulets, dripping down to the electro current beneath, the electric hissing as droplets hit the wires, the scent of warm iron wafting up to her as she climbed.

"It's a castle, a bouncy razor castle, and I'll bleed if you make me, bleed, bleed, bleed... Let's bring out the cake and blow the candles out, I need help and I'm shouting out with doubt..."

The words spurned her on to move, her brain racing with questions…*What happened when the song ended? Who was singing? Why did she know the voice? Why was she here? Was she going to die?*

She was so determined to reach the other side and away with her own thoughts that she didn't see the razors that had been glued to the last section of rope until it was too late. Her feet seared in sharp pain as the blades sliced her skin open, the razors digging in harshly to her toes, feeling as if they would be amputated off. The shock took her out of her trance, but she wasn't quick enough to react as her body reflexively let go and she began to fall…

"Wrap me up and open me like a present, you're all Lords and Ladies, and I'm a peasant, tell me why the bunting drips with blood, is it because mine is mud now?"

The lyrics swayed around her as she fell, time seemed to slow down as she could hear the buzzing come for her.

ZZZZZZZZZAAAAAAAAAPPPPPPPPP!

The electrical current from the car batteries zipped and zapped through her body as she landed on the walkway of lightning. The pain rippled through her body as the shock of the current launched her back into the air and she was flung like a rag doll onto the soft mat of the play area floor.

She flopped down hard, her body jerking from the memory and left over current in her system and within her. As it subsided and she lay motionless her eyes fluttered shut and she heard the verse of the song…

"Maybe this is a prank for me…

Again now… Again now…

Death's Carousel

Maybe the name Skank for me...

Is not the worst now... the worst now..." The song danced in her brain with an almost dream like feel. Her body felt tight and sore yet charged and burnt. She tried to stay awake, but her body felt broken. Her eyes fluttered one last time before she remembered...

     *   *   *

Balloons decorated the large archway that led to Leanne's sweet sixteenth birthday celebration. It was being held in the back garden of Leanne's family home, it was a large estate with a seven bedroomed Victorian style house, a double garage, and a vast garden that extended for acres. A swimming pool sat with pool floaties and a makeshift *'mocktail'* bar and a table set up with nibbles, party food and a chocolate fountain. A boombox had been set up to one side of the garden, along with a huge adult sized bouncy castle.

Sinead sighed as she was dropped off on the huge driveway where Leanne's parents 4x4's sat, their paint work polished and shining in the warmth of the sun's rays. Leanne didn't know how lucky she was, her family lived like reality television stars, with their large fully furnished home, decorated accordingly with how celebrities would style their homes to a stupidly high spec of the moment. Marbled flooring covered the front entry and into a large foyer like room with grand staircases leading up to the first floor. Potted plants and large palms greeted you as you headed through into the kitchen. Sinead's favourite room was the kitchen with its vast amount of granite work tops, double oven and island complete with sink and coffee pod machine. Sinead loved to cook, and a kitchen like this would have been a dream, but Leanne's family rarely used it, choosing to take out or dine out as a dinner option as they didn't want to ruin the look of the unlived in kitchen.

Then there was Queen Leanne's master bedroom with ensuite and walk in wardrobe. It had been decorated in a crushed velvet theme, the curtains, the bed, the vanity table and chair and the rug, all silver and crushed velvet. Along with a makeup set up fit for a fully qualified celebrity makeup artist.

Sinead loved Leanne, she was her bestie, but she did envy her lifestyle and found her bratty behaviour to be tiresome at times. But their mums were also good friends, and Leanne's parents knew people, such as a modelling agency that Sinead and her mum wanted her to sign to. So, it was always best to keep on her good side, even when she was being 'Queen Brat of Bratsville'.

As Sinead walked under the archway and headed down the garden path to find her best friend, she jangled the bag of goodies she had for her. She filled it with presents on the top, a cute teddy, some perfume and her favourite lip gloss, but underneath she had hidden a bottle of Vodka, some vapes and some reasonably sharp objects. Leanne had informed her that her parents had made her invite the freaky girl from school, the one who looked like a dead vampire and who's clothes were way to big and untrendy, the one who had been a laughingstock on the Carousel ride. Together they had hatched a plan to attack the girl, make her bleed for her crime of existing.

Death's Carousel

Sinead cheerily sauntered into the garden, Leanne's face lit up and she ran over to her shrieking with joy.

"Here's your present baby girl", She said handing over the bag full of goodies.

"Did you bring the stuff?" Leanne asked glancing into the bag and smiling at the glint of silver wrapped in tissue paper at the bottom.

"Sure did", she smirked, "What's the plan?"

Leanne filled her in as they walked through the crowd of party goers, the music boomed all around her and the smell of chocolate made her stomach rumble. She took a look at the chocolate fountain, licking her lips in anticipation… But she stepped away, she had to watch her figure, eating crap would scarper her chances of joining the modelling agency that her mum had set up a meeting for. She'd been on a strict diet and working out intensely for weeks, she didn't want a drop of chocolate to ruin it… "A moment on the lips lasts a lifetime on the hips", her mums voice sounded in her mind, a constant reminder to not pig out.

As they walked past the food they made their way to the bouncy castle, Leanne had already informed other guests not to use it as they had a prank planned for the ugly freak. It was empty as they approached, and the girls set out to work. Leanne's mum glanced over seeing the girls on the castle and beamed that they were using it, she had insisted her daughter have one for a laugh, saying it was the last year she could 'baby' her.

Her mum heard the doorbell ring, and she walked off in her Louis Vuitton stiletto heels, the red shining out from under the heel, like a beacon for what was to come.

A few moments later they were finished, just as Leanne's mum came out and called her over... The freak had arrived!

Kayella stood as if she was trying to wrap in on herself, her arms hugged her slender frame, her hair enveloping her in a blanket of darkness as it always did. She was wearing a dress, it looked handmade and screamed cheap to Leanne.

"What is she wearing?" Leanne whispered to Sinead as they got closer.

Sinead for a moment had been admiring the handmade garment, the dress was purple and shaped into her waist and then flowed out like a watery, silky fabric. The top had been cut to frame her slender neck and collar bones and dipped slightly to reveal a pretty heart locket. A pretty purple mesh with sparkles on had been sewn into the top, again it gave an almost airy, watery look to the dress. Then she wore cute black kitten heels, and had some makeup on, a bit of blush to flush her cheeks, a dash of shimmering eyeshadow and mascara and a glossy lip. Other than her awkward stance, the girl looked pretty.

Sinead almost said out loud that she liked the look but caught herself before it left her lips. She really didn't want to upset her bestie today of all days, she would never be able to live it down... Ever!

"Oh, god it looks... so... Cheap", she exclaimed, and Leanne nodded in agreement.

As they approached, they spotted Kayella's nan, she had dropped her off and was talking to Leanne's mum and dad, "Yes, she's doing well now, especially since the Carousel incident at the fairground... She loves to sing and has a beautiful little voice, so she got herself a little job down at the Record Store to pay for some professional lessons with Janice McQueen… You know, the old music teacher from the college".

Leanne's parents nodded and seemed to approve of the story being told, "Oh, that sounds lovely, well-done Kayella".

Kayella smiled shyly but her smile dropped when she saw the two girls approaching her safe space.

Her nan reached forward and handed her a gift bag, Kayella grasped it with nervous hands, the bag shivering from side to side.

"Oh Leanne, Kayella's here. Doesn't she look beautiful… Her nan said Kayelle made the dress herself out of some material she found… Isn't it wonderful… And she sings now… Janice McQ…"

"Yeah, yeah great", Leanne cut her mum off mid-sentence, "Come on Fr… Er… Kayella, let's go". The word freak had nearly left her mouth, and Sinead had to stifle a giggle at the near miss that could have got her into tonnes of trouble.

Leanne had blamed the fair ground incident on Nancy, even filmed it to keep her name clear and squeaky clean. Nancy had been grounded for months and had to miss out on the party as her parents pretty much had her under house arrest, they believed the demon that made her do it would get bored and leave. So, a little slip up would have her party cancelled in a heartbeat and people realising Nancy hadn't done it alone.

Leanne took Kayella's arm and whisked her off into the throng of the party. Kayella felt rigid with fear, but she must have felt a little safer with Leanne and Sinead than normal as she didn't try to pull away like she had at the fair. *Maybe it was because the adults were overseeing the whole event? Maybe she thought they wouldn't try anything?* Whatever her reasons Leanne laughed inside at the stupidity of the girl who they were about to prank… Big Style!

Kayella handed the bag with a birthday gift to Leanne, her timid face worrying at what she would say in regard to her present but hope also filled her eyes as their hands exchanged the bag, a hope that her gift would be accepted, well received, and things would start to change. But things never change, Leanne didn't even look, just dismissing it and placing it on a table nearby and walked away from it without a second thought or glance.

The threesome of girls headed off towards the main bash, balloons bounced around as some people kicked them about to one another. Just as Leanne was about to lead Kayella to the bouncy castle her mum called her over, another guest had arrived. She huffed but told Kayella to stay put as she and Sinead went off to meet and greet.

Kayella stood by the edge of the party taking everything in, it was unreal. No one had ever really invited her to a birthday party before, only Nancy and that had been more out of pity and her parents suggesting it and even then, it was more low key, so certain people wouldn't see or know Kayella had been invited. Other than that, no parties, not from other so-called friends, nor her non-existent family… So, this was, something new. She kind of liked it, the sweet smells of all the food, the noise of people talking and having fun. The hum of the music and the colours, all the balloons and decorations, it was cool. And then there was the hugest pile of presents Kayella had ever seen in her life! It was magical… A fantasy!

"Hey?" A cool, kind and familiar voice said from behind her.

She turned to see the boy who had helped her on the carousel ride. She instantly felt her cheeks flush red, "Oh…Hi", she tried to half smile, but it felt weird, *no one ever talked to her willingly, let alone a boy… A boy who she knew Leanne liked a lot.*

"Remember me?" he asked looking a tad confused by her reaction.

She nodded, "Yeah, you helped me… Tristan, right?"

It was his turn to nod, "Yeah… Er… Sorry about what Lee and Nancy did to you, it wasn't nice but… She was led on by Nancy. Leanne can be nice, she just… Can be easily led… Er… You know what I mean…" He stopped midway through, he clearly didn't know what else to say.

Kayella half smiled and nodded but began to back off from him, clearly Leanne had brainwashed him into believing that rubbish. But she knew, she knew Nancy didn't lead her on, it was the other way around. Her and Nancy had been friends before, until she began to get feelings for her nemesis. But Nancy didn't have the smarts to outwit Leanne or come up with such a grand prank idea… *Oh no, that was definitely 'Lee's' department!*

He held up his hands, "I'm sorry I didn't mean to upset you… Leanne has been a… Bitch to you, I know she has I just… I'm sorry". His soft brown eyes met hers and

Kayella felt a fuzzy feeling in her stomach, kind of nausea and excitement.

She nodded again but didn't say anything.

"You wanna grab a drink?" he asked.

"Sure", she said quietly.

He led her away from where she was meant to stay and wait, and they made their way to a large table full of food and drink. A punch bowl was on one table, it was a funny peachy colour, and it smelt like alcohol... *Surely the parents wouldn't allow this at a sixteenth birthday? The sign said 'Mocktails'...*

Tristan took two of the plastic cups and filled them up to the brim, his eyes smiling and motioning to under the table where empty and discarded vodka bottles sat, semi hidden but not very well. *So, the parents had no idea?*

He took a sip and pulled a face, "Shit that is strong haha". He then looked at her and egged her on to drink.

She took a sip, she felt the warmth of the alcohol go down her throat, the fruity taste of the punch was sugary sweet, it went down too easily, and Kayella wanted more. She took a bigger sip and giggled nervously at Tristan.

"It's good right?"

She nodded in reply.

"Come on let's go find somewhere to sit".

They walked through the crowd of teenagers that were slowly and surely getting merry in the warm suns after glow. The garden was huge and spanned for acres and Tristan led her down a path away from the noise of the party, but not too far away. He could sense she was nervous by the way she kept looking back.

"It's ok you're with me", he smiled.

Death's Carousel

"I...Er...Was meant to wait for Leanne and Sinead over there", She said shyly, "I wasn't meant to move from that spot".

"They'll find us, plus, what's a party if you're just going to stand there. We should all be having fun", his eyes beamed into hers, almost melting away any fears she had. They were soft, kind and trusting. And although she desperately wanted to trust him, she found it so hard to let down her guard.

"Yeah... Maybe", she smiled with a shy ache.

"Let's sit here, under some shade", he motioned to under a big tree. Its vibrant green leaves made the perfect umbrella, the perfect shady spot. They sat there for a while, the party going on behind them. For once Kayella felt calm, connected and listened to. She didn't say too much, but when she did Tristan seemed to listen to her every word intently, nodding at the right time, laughing when needed and looking into her eyes... No one ever looked at her eyes, no one ever looked at her like she was a real person. They only ever saw her as the freak.

She didn't know if it was the drink, or whether she actually was beginning to trust him and relax, but she felt her worries drift away momentarily, she felt the cool breeze filter through the tree's leaves and wash over her, she felt at ease, she didn't want it to end.

Leanne's hawk eyes were raging. She felt like spitting feathers, running over to where the two teenage girls spied the freak and Tristan having a lovely summer day walk and chat under the tree, very romantic indeed. But instead, she was stuck playing the 'Good' girl, greeting her cousins and aunts and uncles as they arrived to celebrate her party, forced by her mum to take photos and smile, all the while the freak was with him... Tristan, her Tristan.

Sinead pulled Leanne back like the little Jack Russel she was. She growled obscenities under her breath so her parents couldn't hear, but they were all aimed at the freak girl now sitting blissfully unaware with Leanne's man, the man Leanne had her eye on and her claws nearly into.

"How dare she?" Leanne growled, a pure hatred vibrating through her veins.

Sinead watched as Kayella sat under the tree, she looked different, happy, she chatted away to Tristan, his dark eyes all over her, a beam of happiness spread over his dark features. Kayella used her hands a lot to communicate, like a hyperactive child. If it hadn't been the freaky girl Sinead would have found it cute, bittersweet and...

Leanne grabbed Sinead's arm snapping her out of her thoughts, "Now, it happens now!"

Sinead paused for a moment still looking at the girl, a cutesy little girly giggle passed her lips, her cheeks rosy, red from blushing and consuming alcohol, her teeth glinting in the sunlight, her once buckteeth now straightened from the braces that lined her mouth. Sinead almost felt a pang of guilt, maybe in another life they could have been friends, she was creative, made her own clothes, a fashionista in the making, someone Sinead could have been friends with, discussed fashion ideas with... But... Leanne... Leanne was the boss, she ruled the roost, she made the rules, and no one messed with the rules. And as Leanne and her own mum were teaching her, sometimes you needed to be ruthless and step on or over people to get what and where you wanted.

Leanne's mum ushered the family away and let Leanne go to enjoy her party, and for her it couldn't happen quick enough. She stormed across the green grass, crushing daisies and buttercups underfoot. Tristan spotted Leanne before Kayella did, his eyes widened with concern, the look on her face full of disgust. Kayella turned to where his eyes looked, her happy, smiley expression faltering to a withered sadness. Sinead felt that pang of guilt again, that sadness… it was… heartbreakingly beautiful. She just had to keep telling herself that the girl deserved it, if Leanne willed it to be, then so it should be. Sinead couldn't turn soft now, she could not lose her cool, could not lose her validation and chances, by being friends with Leanne those were things she could provide.

"Get up", she shrieked.

"Sorry", Kayella whispered, her eyes wondered to Tristan and then to Sinead, pleading for something, anything as she got to her feet.

"As you're here ruining my day you can at least be helpful", Leanne hissed through gritted teeth.

"Helpful?" Kayella said softly.

"Yeah… The bouncy castle, someone threw one of my presents in there, but I won't be seen dead in one of those, they are for kids! You can retrieve it for me".

"Ok", she replied and went to move, but Tristan grabbed her arm.

"Get it yourself, she's not your maid", he retorted.

A look of shock and anger crossed Leanne's face, her eyes narrowing, "What?"

"You heard... Get it yourself", he snapped and grabbed Kayella's hand and walked her away from the two dumbstruck girls.

Leanne shook with anger, Sinead thought she could see actual steam leak from her ears. Then she turned to her, "And you..." She snapped accusingly.

Sinead stepped back, "What have I done?"

"You didn't back me... And I saw the way you looked at her, you pity her, you feel sorry for her! Well don't... You are my friend, so start acting like it. Now, find a way to bring her to the bouncy castle".

"Or what?" Sinead quipped crossing her arms standing her ground.

"Or those bra pic's you sent to Morgan Dean will be plastered all over the school and I'll get my mum to leave a little note with the modelling company about the pic's too... They won't want a troublesome model".

Leanne spun on her heel and left Sinead feeling defeated. She forgot she had access to those. For some reason Leanne demanded she have access to all her *'Besties'* social media accounts *'Or they weren't true friends'*, unfortunately that meant she saw all their deepest and darkest secrets and used them often as weapons. Sinead watched Tristan and Kayella walked back up to the house heading to the drinks again. Sighing, she followed.

Sinead waited for a while, hovering nearby but not close enough for Tristan or Kayella to sense her presence. Leanne stood with Marielle, Luke, Mario and a few other people, one being a cute guy called Leon something or other, a boy two years their senior who Leanne had a major crush on, and so did Sinead, but he wasn't interested in 'Little girls' but apparently loved a good party.

Out of the corner of her eye she could see that Leanne was keeping tabs on her progress. She was about to give up and beg her not to expose her when Tristan walked off into the house leaving Kayella holding both drinks. Clearly, he needed a pit stop.

She took her chance and headed over to the lone girl, "Hey… Kayella, I love your dress".

The girl half smiled but had her guard up, "Thanks".

"Come, come talk with me, I'd love to know what fabric you used and what stitch work you done, it's almost seamless".

Kayella replied, "I used a sewing machine, it done the stitches…"

Duh! Sinead could see she wasn't getting anywhere with her fast, and time was of the essence as Tristan would be back soon. "Look girl I really need your help. Leanne is still kicking off about the present inside the bouncy castle and she's making my life hell over it. I offered to get it but apparently, I can't be seen doing that for her… It's a 'Hierarchy' thing or something!" She paused using her fingers to make quotation marks, "But, if you could get it for me, it would mean we could start accepting you into the group… I mean you'd start at the bottom of the hierarchy of course but like me, you can work your way up". Sinead knew it sounded like bullshit, but she had to try something.

Kayella sighed and put the drinks down on the table, "Fine, but I know your lying".

"What girl? No… I'm not lying, na ah".

Kayella just pulled a face, rolling her eyes a little and started walking to the bouncy castle. Sinead had never seen this annoyance in her before, it threw her a little, maybe the drink was giving the girl some balls. She was at the castle in seconds and Leanne's face was peering out through the crowd with a smile and anticipation. She tried to loosely place her arm through Leon's to try and get his attention, to entrap him like the Black Widow she was and would become. But he pulled away, turning back to his friends. Annoyance crossed her face again, but she couldn't hold in her excitement for what was to come for the freak.

The girls had rigged the bouncy castle, placed razors and sharp objects all along the bit where you climb in and out, but it was hidden under a thick cushion. Kayella climbed in over the cushion, not noticing the sharps beneath. Sinead whisked the cushion away as soon as the girl had vanished inside and waited, holding her breath, a feeling of dread and amusement filling her body, adrenaline making her heart flutter. She knew it was wrong, it was nasty, but all she wanted was to be one of the popular girls, to be accepted and to get to where she wanted to be. She wanted and needed Leanne to still want her as a friend, this would prove her loyalty for sure, she would not be a nobody again.

"There's nothing in here", Kayella called out.

"Oh, oopsie my mistake", Sinead grinned at the group that had descended upon the castle.

Kayella began to climb out, her eyes looking up and out at the group that were all staring at her intently, not down at where her hands were going.

Slice…

Death's Carousel

A look of searing pain crossed Kayella's soft features, her dark eyes welling up with tears of pain and betrayal. She let out a soft wail and lifted up her hands, both of them had been sliced open by the razors that had been crudely taped onto the bouncy castle's entrance. Crying out with more pain she clambered over the entrance and fell to the floor, the pain and sight of blood causing her to feel dizzy and sick. She tried to stand, but her legs kept buckling beneath her, she placed one bloody handprint on her knee trying to lever herself to a standing position.

Sinead looked at Leanne, her smile faltering, Leanne looked pissed, clearly the girl wasn't creating enough of a ruckus, Leanne had wanted a show, to make a spectacle of the freak. Flushes of heat filled Sinead's cheeks, she needed to do something, to add to the girl's humiliation so Leanne would forgive her and keep her secret. Looking around for anything that would do she stopped and smiled.

"Oh, my Kayella what happened? You really shouldn't harm yourself it's not clean... Here let me help you wash up", Sinead grabbed the girl by her hair and then pushed and shoved Kayella into the pool. A Quick splash and the water began to turn red, like hundreds of hungry piranha had been sitting in wait for a meal.

Kayella desperately tried to swim but her hands refused to work, her brain fogging over in the panic, her body stinging with pain as the chemicals in the pool cleansed her wounds. She slowly stopped thrashing, she gave up, gave in, *maybe she should just give up entirely...* Sinead mused, *make my life one hundred times easier with Lee.*

Then warm, strong arms embraced Kayella, strong yet caring hands gripped her shoulders and hauled her out of the pool. A few theatrical screams ripened the air as people pretended to not know what was going on as she was laid to rest on floor. Her dark wet hair billowed out around her, as did her blood that began to pool around her hands, mixing in with her long hair, a bloody darkness in which enveloped her.

"Who did this? Who did it?" Tristan shouted at the group, his top clinging to his wet muscular body.

Leanne's parents came running down, one with towels and another on the phone to the ambulance.

Tristan shouted again, "Who did this to her?" and he pointed at the razors lazily taped to the bouncy castle. His eyes flashed over to Leanne, but like the award-winning actress she was, she was in floods of tears, bawling her eyes out. She knelt by Kayella sobbing, resting a hand on her shoulder. Everyone else stayed quiet.

"Maybe she did it herself for attention?" Sinead offered.

Tristan turned to her, "What?"

She shrugged, "Maybe she didn't like the attention not being on her, maybe she did it for attention?"

He shook his head, "It was you, wasn't it? You did this to her?"

She pretended to look shocked, to feign surprise, but she wasn't the actress Leanne was, and everyone saw straight through her, or chose to side against her, "No… No… Not me… I was… I was with Leanne".

Death's Carousel

"We saw you walking with her not two minutes ago", Leanne's dad said, "Lee was with some other friends".

She opened her mouth and closed it, *shit, there was no way out of this one…*

Two months after the party Sinead had finally been allowed back to Leanne's house. Lee's parents had banned her for a while but eventually events like that get forgotten and life moves on. Sinead had protested that it was a moment of madness, she was stressed out over their upcoming exams and that she fancied Tristan, but Kayella had been flirting with him, and it made her mad. *And the girl didn't die, no harm done right?* None of it true of course… Leanne was the one who fancied Tristan and Leon and Morgan and most of the boys in their year group and beyond. Plus, Sinead held no stress over exams, for she was going to be a model, and she didn't need English, Maths or Science for that, all she needed was her good looks and her legs.

Kayella on the other hand was still healing. One of the slices had cut so deep down into her muscle that her hand wasn't working properly… Her chances of a sewing or fashion career most probably ruined…

But it didn't matter, Sinead was back in everyone's good books, the horror of what happened to the freaky girl forgotten… Everything that happened to her was always conveniently forgotten… And Sinead knew her own career was going to be just fine.

* * *

"It's a castle, a bouncy razor castle, and I'll bleed if you make me, bleed, bleed, bleed… Let's bring out the cake and blow the candles out… I need help and I'm feeling washed with doubt…"

The verse was sung twice, a sort of finality to the song as Sinead came round. Her head throbbed from the pain of being electrocuted, parts of her body screamed and stung from the sharp incisions.

She hadn't always been ruthless, she had grown to not care what others thought, just about where she wanted to be in life, and she no longer cared for who she had to walk over to get it. She wanted, desired, no… Deserved to be at the top of her game.

But now she was trapped in Kayella's game… It just had to be her. Kayella loved to sing, she had the sweetest voice, she remembered from music classes at school, the teacher always made Kayella sing, especially on open evenings to show off the school's talent… But also, the bouncy castle, the razors, the sharps, it's all what Sinead had done to her that fateful day… *But there was no water here, no swimming pool, maybe Kayella would let her go? To just keep this between them?*

Tears rolled silently down Sinead's cheeks, Kayella had done nothing to her to make her bully her, hell, she'd done nothing to Leanne either, but Leanne just had this rage, this automatic hatred for her. Sinead laughed to herself, what made things worse was that Leanne had gone to college and was now studying psychology at University to become a Therapist, apparently, she wanted to help people now, she was a changed woman. She wanted to listen, to advise, to be... kind. *How on Earth could she believe she could do that, especially when she caused so much trauma to another human being?*

A figure appeared before her as she lay broken and helpless on the floor. She tried to move but only her fingers danced wildly, the rest of her body was in a hibernating slumber. The figure wore a long dark cloak, the hood up over her head as if to mimic the Grim Reaper herself. She stood above Sinead, her dark eyes peering out from beneath the cloak.

"I'm sorry", Sinead whispered, but she knew there was nothing she could say to fix or change things.

"Are you? Are you really sorry? Or just sorry that you're here, in this predicament?" Kayella's soft floating voice had taken a cool and calm tone, it sounded threatening, and it made Sinead's skin prickle with goosebumps.

"I am sorry, so, so, so, sorry for what we did to you", She felt so weak as she spoke, it took all her strength to pronounce the few words.

"You're so sorry... but you weren't when..." she stopped the sentence and began to sing the last few words, "I'm bleeding, I'm dying, you're killing me, I'm crying".

Sinead felt it, the end of the song was mere syllables away, and she could feel it too, that the end was nearly here for her.

As Kayella sang the bloody words in a soft, but powerful tone she lifted the mic and pushed a button hidden within the hilt. A mechanical click sounded, and Sinead looked up. On the ceiling of the play area was a large tub, some sort of device held it in place. The click sounded again, and the tub began to tip, a couple of drops of red water splashed out over her. The netting of the play area would offer no protection from the fluid that was about to rain down over her.

Kayella leant forward and whispered into Sinead's ear, "I'm bleeding, I'm dying, you're killing me… I'm crying". Then she stepped back as the full flood of the reddened liquid cascaded over her. Sinead tried to move but her broken body refused, and she could do nothing as the liquid filled up her mouth, her nose and eventually her lungs. She tried to cough but she couldn't cough hard enough to evacuate the killing fluid. She coughed and twitched, the water drowning her… her body felt weak, her lungs raw… her eyes glassy.

"I'm bleeding, I'm dying, you're killing me, I'm crying… It's a castle, a bouncy razor castle… and I'll bleed If you make me… bleed, bleed, bleed… Let's bring out the cake and blow the candles out… I need help and I'm shouting out with doubt… It's a castle, a bouncy razor castle… It's a castle…a bouncy…razor…CASTLE".

As the last word was sung, Sinead slipped away, her soul cleansed and washed away from her body.

*

The song ended and Kayella lowered the mic, her second performance of the night and it went just as well as the first. Sinead lay in a pool of red water and her own blood from the cuts. Her body was still twitching, her eyes open and unseeing, the life draining from her like water being pulled from the plug in a bath.

Death's Carousel

Kayella stared at the girl beneath her feet, she had thought she would feel some sort of guilt or shame for what she had done and what she was doing, but no, nothing, she felt elated at her revenge, her closure over Sinead being the second one to die by her hand, the way she had been the one terrorised by her hand, by all their dirty, grubby little hands.

She smiled as she swiftly turned and headed to a door at the other end of the play zone, one hidden by the vast thing that was the deflating bouncy castle. She hurried along, passing through one door then another, finally coming to a room that was dark but highlighted by computer screens hooked up to the old CCTV system that the old fairground operators had left behind. Some cameras outside had been left operational by the security company, a security measure to keep trespassers out, or at least a deterrent. But, with some help Kayella had found a way to bypass the security settings, to film her show, her performances, *'their'* performances… Her 'teacher' had taught her many things in life, but this beat all of them. They were a programming genius and hacking into an out-of-date system had been a walk in the park. Turning off the sensors without alerting the security company had been a little trickier, and scoping out the place for weeks, testing the sensors, watching for people that may come to check on the place, but luckily for them the place was well and truly abandoned, even by the security firm being paid to keep an eye on it.

The cameras outside had been rigged, a patch of time filmed, and then replayed again, so if watched back it would look like no one had entered the premises. The camera's throughout had been rigged up to a new system, one where they could access it and watch, it filmed nothing, unless she told it to, but it meant she could watch things unfurling before her, but no evidence… That was key, no evidence and no loose ends! Unless she desired certain evidence to be… Revealed.

She reached the monitors and peered into the one that was next on her performance schedule.

"You did well", a male voice said softly beside her, he sat in a chair watching all the monitors. Watching the show but also keeping watch out for any… intruders that may come looking.

"Thank you", she smiled the smile really reaching her eyes.

He looked away from her, a flash of fear passed through his dark, soft, kind eyes, they didn't mirror her happiness. But she wasn't worried, he had agreed to this, he had owed her, he was her bitch now. She had things held over him, if you wanted to do people dirty then you have to play dirty, they had all taught her that.

At the beginning of her transformation, she had felt shame at the change, she felt her kind, caring, quiet soul leaving her body, being replaced by the revenge seeking banshee. But now, now she was so far gone she didn't care. If she got caught, she had nothing to lose, no family, no friends, no life… But this… This would fix everything, it would give her life, give her the confidence to be who she was truly meant to be, give her the revenge she so deserved for all the years of pain and suffering. And after today her life was going to change in one way or another. Once this was over, she was out, out of this damn, stinking, rotting town, she was flying to the sun, to warmth and happiness to her new life… her new career. Things were already in motion, this was just her last loose end to tidy up so she could move on. And if all failed and something went wrong, well, she knew she had her revenge and that she truly could die happy knowing that, or even if she had to rot in a cell for the rest of her life, she would sleep easy knowing that all those that wronged her were gone. *Why should they be allowed happy lives when they had destroyed hers to the brink of a breakdown. Causing her to become a mere shell of a person, causing her to have an eating disorder, causing her to have mental health issues, causing her to want to cut, copy and paste her body and soul into a new one. They deserved to pay for what they done.* She thought to herself, her whole-body seething with rage, agony and anguish.

    "Are you ready for the next one?" the male voice asked, his hand hovering over a button.

    She nodded, "Are you?"

Chapter Three ... Portaloo Playdate ...

    The Carousel was quiet, deathly quiet. The group of friends all sat on their respected horses and carts waiting. Not one of them wanted to talk, no one wanted to acknowledge that their friend had just been murdered in the most horrendous way. No one said anything in case it set off something else, something that may come for them all.

    Some of them looked around cautiously, not wanting movement to attract attention but what they couldn't see was the hidden CCTV camera operating behind some overgrown leafy foliage by a boarded-up section of wall. The original fairground had been built at the edge of a riverside plot, a high chain link fence was all that separated the back end to the river. The sides of the fairground plot had false walls and panelling, jagged barbed wire and anti-climb paint had been placed all along the top to prevent intruders. The front originally had a semi built front where a ticket station was housed, it had been panelled and gated off. There was no easy escape, and the depressed group knew it, they knew they were trapped.

The camera watched them intently, its flashing green eye taking in each and every one of them. It moved on a hinge that held it in place, focusing on its next victim. The person controlling it gently pressing a button.

CLICK!

Marielle Coppard jumped out of her skin as a panel from above opened and a lone key fell out, dangling mere inches from her face on thin fishing line. The noise had sent her heart hammering into overdrive, that noise had been what killed Nancy, and now she had feared that noise had been her death sentence. But as she let out a breath that she had been holding in she saw that it could be her life sentence. *Maybe whoever was doing this had just meant to kill Nancy and frighten the rest of us…?* She thought, but something nagged inside her, telling her to not rest on that foolish hope, that this was only the beginning.

She snatched up the key and tried it in her cuffs, jumping again as they popped open and crashed loudly to the metal flooring. The loud clang had forced shocked gasps from her friends around her, and although she wanted to help them all straight away, there was one person who needed her help first, Mario, her big brother. She jumped down from her horse and cautiously made her way over the ride to where her brother lay. He had come semi around, laying awkwardly in a carriage that a horse would pull, but the lost look in his eyes told her enough, that he had been awake enough to know Nancy had perished.

"Hey bro, let's get you out", she whispered carefully, placing the key in the lock and grabbing them off him before they could fall to the floor.

His haunted eyes looked at her as he launched into a bear hug, his large arms wrapping around his sister, "What the hell sis, what is this?"

She shrugged as she pulled away and clambered down to go and help one of the others, "I...I don't know".

Within minutes she had them all free, and all of them went to stand to pay Nancy their respects. Mario had his arm around Marielle, tears streaming down his muscular dark features. Marielle just stared but her brain found it hard to place all the images together properly. Nancy sat, pierced in place on her horse, her now dank blonde hair turning to a washed out almost faded pink from the crimson red that spewed from her innards. Her mouth forever frozen open by the deep throated golden spear that penetrated bone and flesh. Her eyes glassed over but forever stuck in fear at what fell from above.

Mario gave a sob from beside her, she felt bad for the big man crying, he wasn't normally one for wearing emotions on his sleeve. But he had loved Nancy, but unfortunately Nancy hadn't felt the same, he was after all the wrong sex for her taste. Marielle felt bad for her brother, Nancy had at times led him on, let him believe that one day there could be a chance if she defected from batting for the other team. But she also felt bad for her friend, she wasn't a bad person, she hadn't deserved this.

Leanne and Jared stood the other side of them, Leanne's normally perfectly made-up face was sliding, raccoon eyes bled black down her cheeks from her mascara, her tears running black, white and grey streaks down her face and neck as they washed away her foundation leaving slug like trails behind. Her eyes red and blotchy, her caramel hair ruffled and frizzy from the cooling and now damp night air. Any warmth from the day was filtering away, and the clouds were threatening to cry with them, mourning their friend.

Jared stood there almost emotionless, not a single tear fell, but fear swallowed his tongue as he found he couldn't speak, the shock was all too much.

"Why? Why would someone do this?" Mario's deep voice coming back from his emotional softness.

"They're sick whoever they are", Leanne said.

"Why Nancy though, and why us?" Marielle asked.

Jared stood there for a moment, still shell shocked until he calmly stated, "We need to get out of here, it's not safe".

They all looked at him, he was clearly stating the obvious, but someone had to say it.

Mario nodded, "Yeah bro we do". He began to look around the decaying fairground, the only lighting was coming from the flashing carousel lights and a few single spotlights dotted around on the false wall panelling. He could see the looming shadow of darkness that had once been the Ferris Wheel, but no lights flickered on, it's decaying cage like seats that lifted up into the air were hanging by threads, threatening to fall, smash and burn to the ground with just the smallest gust of wind.

He couldn't see an immediate way out, but they had to try.

He walked over to some wet and splintered chip board that had been stacked up against the chain link fence, using his brute strength he began ripping them apart and throwing them out of his way. If he remembered rightly there had been some old boat rides at the back of the fair, maybe they would still be in working condition to get out.

He flinched and shot back as something dark and slimy moved in the shadows, something large enough to be a small dog, with beady eyes and jagged teeth. It squeaked and bolted out from under his feet. A Rat!

"Shit", he exclaimed jumping further back from the offending rodent.

"Get it away from me", a panicked squeal sounded out from Jared.

Mario turned to look at the weedy man before him, he shuddered with repulsion, his face paling further, "Mate it's just a rat, they ain't nice but…"

"No, get it away, get it away", he shrieked a noise so high pitched even the girls looked bemused. His body recoiling in disgust, he walked backwards knocking over empty cans, wooden boards and a shrub.

"You're in a wonderland of terror and you're freaking out over a rat, man grow up!" Mario said.

"I had a bad experience lately with rats", he hissed, "I… I just can't stand them".

Mario shook his head and went back to where he was before, lifting the boards to look around.

"Wait what's that?" Marielle asked.

They all turned to where she was pointing. A small green light beamed and flashed in the now darkening fair ground. Where Jared had knocked over things, one being a decayed shrub in a plant pot that had been placed lazily to hide something… A camera! There was indeed a camera that was clearly watching them.

"Some sicko is watching us", Mario said leaning down and peering into the lens. He waved and then stuck up his middle finger.

"Don't aggravate them", Marielle said with fear in her voice, she glanced around, "It could anger them".

"They clearly already want us dead Marielle, what does it matter", Leanne smirked.

"Because I at least want a chance to escape, and if not pissing them off ups our chances, then I'm all for it", she replied bluntly.

Leanne shook her head and turned to Jared who was rubbing his own arms as if he was cold, she then rolled her eyes and leant on a more stable wall panel looking at her nails.

Mario leaned back into the camera, grabbed the lens and casing and ripped it from the wall.

"Mario don't", Marielle cried out, but it was too late, he smashed it on the floor and stamped on it.

"What? I ain't having no sick shit watching us", he said, going back once again to the area he found the rat. He picked up a few more debris of the world before, when the fair ground had been a place of fun and life, not fear and death. Finally, a view of the water through the fence appeared but his heart sank, weeds, overgrown brambles and rubbish was strewn around but no boats, a perfect rat house but not the escape he wanted… An idea came to him… *Unless they could all swim?*

"Can you all swim?" He asked casually.

"Yes".
"Yeah".
"No".

The no came from Jared who looked wide eyed and shocked that it had even been asked, "Swim...Swim? What happened to the pedalo boats that used to be here? And I ain't swimming with no rats!"

Marielle answered, "They probably decommissioned them long before the place fully closed down to the public. I remember a few accidents happened with the boats not being properly maintained and people nearly drowning".

"They probably all at the bottom of the lake Bro", Mario added.

"We can't swim across the river", Leanne said shaking her head in disbelief, "Number one, Jared can't swim and number two, it's too far to get to land again even for us stronger swimmers, what if there is a hidden current ready to sweep us away".

Mario spoke, "No it's not too far, plus, we swim close to the edge of the fair, we don't need to go across the big ass pond".

"What? Swim right to the front of this place. What if the bad guys are waiting for us there?"

Leanne cried, "And we can't leave Jared behind".

"Jared can hold onto me", Mario offered, "And the bad guys are waiting for us anyway somewhere, they probably got camera's set up all over the place to watch us. Sick bastards. We need a chance to get out and get as far away as we can".

Death's Carousel

"No…No… I'm not doing it, I'm not swimming, I can't", Jared wheezed in fear. He looked out of the dark lapping waves, the ripples of rubbish bobbing up and down in the darkness, flashes of the growing moonlight peering down on the water, causing what looked like millions of beady eyes to stare at him. The beady eyes being more like the ripples of the water shining back the light, they were washed away as the lapping water flushed away the false imagery. But the fear was there, etched into his mind, the lake was full of them… Rats!

"Then we come back for you, we go get help, find a phone and call the police", Mario suggested, "You could hide somewhere, and wait for help to come".

"I'm not leaving him", Leanne huffed.

"Then you both hide together and wait for the cavalry to come".

"And what if you guys don't make it, and we stay hidden forever and die anyway!" Leanne snapped, "Look, we need to stay together, safety in numbers, right? Someone comes for us, we band together and take them on. When people split up in horror films that's always when people start to die".

"This is not a horror film Lee", Marielle sighed.

"You think we can take on some crazed, singing, murderous lunatic?" Mario laughed, "Bro, they clearly drugged us, got us here and tied us up and pierced Nancy to death. You think we have got a chance, they will probably have the fairground rigged with booby traps, swimming is our only way out".

Leanne went to speak but was cut off by the squeal of door hinges screaming in the darkness. Jared jumped out of his skin almost into her arms. The sound like a hundred squeaking rodents, baying for blood.

They all looked to where the noise had sounded, a lone door swung open, swaying in the cool breeze that ran off the river. *Had it been opened on purpose by their crazed killer? Or had the breeze simply nudged it open?* The door was situated right next to a rusted cotton candy and popcorn machine. Its lights were on, and swirls of mouldy sugar and bugs swirled in the air inside the machine. The machines mechanics sounding almost as shrill as the door's hinges.

Everyone was on high alert, all of them looking at the door, but no one moved or spoke for a moment.

"Oh, hell to this shit", Mario said starting for the fence, "I'm out".

"It could just be the wind", Leanne suggested grabbing Mario's arm, "Let's just check it out, it could be a way out".

"Or it could be the crazy murderer!" He snapped, he reached the fence, was about to put his hand out to touch it.

Marielle felt uneasy, and she was sure a new noise was sounding, like a faint electrical hum, "Mario wait!" she cried out, but it was too late.

His hand touched the fence, and a huge shock rocked his body, his body shook and trembled with energy, his fingers twitching open and closed, then open enough to let go and he fell back to the floor with a thud.

"Mario!" He could hear his sisters worried voice but couldn't make his mouth work to say anything.

Marielle ran to his side, her worried face looking over his. Whilst she tended to him Jared walked over to the fence and looked through. Sure enough, the other side had a car battery tied with wires to the fence to make it electrified.

"Electric fence", Jared said, "They don't want us to go that way… Too easy".

Leanne huddled up to Jared, true fear written all over her face, "I told him we shouldn't go that way".

Marielle looked up at her annoyed, "This isn't a 'I told you so' moment Lee, he's hurt".

She looked down at her brother, he was still conscious, but the shock had caused his body to go into a kind of limp mode, like a car that needed a service, just the bare minimum working to keep him alive.

"Is he ok? Can he walk?" Jared asked Marielle.

She shrugged and pulled at her brother's arm, he started to sit up, slowly. After a few more minutes of trying, she managed to get him to his feet. He leaned on her, his breathing slow, "Let's go, fuck this, I want out", he breathed.

"You sure?" she asked him, her long afro hair bobbing as she manoeuvred her arm to give him more of her shoulder to support him.

"Yeah, like I said… I want out", sweat had beaded on his top lip as he spoke.

"Ok, then let's go", she said. At least if they got out sooner rather than later, she could get him to a hospital, get him the help he needed.

The group headed to the door, Jared taking lead, Leanne just behind followed by Marielle holding up Mario. Jared cautiously walked into a long corridor, it was dark and one lone hanging light swung from the decrepit, crumbling rafters. It cast an eerie glow down the corridor, the light bouncing off the damp, mould covered walls. They walked down checking random doors as they reached them, but they were all locked. Jared had tried kicking one of them, but he wasn't built for strength, his skinny weedy legs barely holding up his scared frail frame. *Mario had been the one for strength, he could have kicked the door down,* Marielle thought to herself, but he was in no condition to do so now. So, they kept walking, trying more doors until one finally opened.

The door at the end opened into, a toilet block… A dead end! Marielle felt exasperated at the sight of the flooded room. It stunk, literally smelt like shit. All the toilet cubicle doors were smashed off revealing blocked and damaged toilets. All had overflowed rancid waste that was awash all over the tiled floor, but the sewage water was deep enough that Marielle couldn't tell what type or colour the tiles were.

"Over here!" Leanne called out.

They all looked to see in one corner was another door, disguised by the wall having rotted away to the same black mouldy colour as the walls. She pulled the handle, but it wouldn't budge.

Jared walked over and wiped his sleeve over a brass name plate that was congealed on the door, '*Cleaning Cupboard*'. He sighed, "It's a dead end".

Leanne looked down at her feet, disappointed.

Marielle looked around the rest of the room, a small slit of a window was above the wall with some smashed sinks set into a sideboard and four shattered mirrors, but it wasn't big enough to fit a person through.

Death's Carousel

"What about that? Behind the last cubicle?" Mario breathed beside her.

Jared looked to where Mario pointed, there was a hole in the wall.

"Can you check it out?" Mario asked him.

He felt his throat tighten, he didn't want to, but Mario couldn't do it, and the girls were depending on him. He nodded, swallowed and leant down to look.

It was the height of a child but quite wide, wide enough for someone to fit through, but it was dark and gloomy ahead and he couldn't see what was beyond his own hand as he reached inside. He leant down further and began to climb through, his body recoiling in disgust at the squidgy sludge that clung to his lower body. A few cobwebs caught on his face as he tried to stand up the other side, he felt panic rise, a sick feeling from his fear, but he wanted out of this place. Using his hands to feel around and to make sure he didn't hit his head. The wall was damp and cold beneath his touch, but as he stared into the gloom, he could see a small spec of light, another door!

"Anything?" Mario's voice boomed in the darkness, he was sounding stronger by the minute.

"I think there's a door", Jared called out, "Let me check it". He made his way, sloshing in the cold yuck around him. Reaching the door, he pushed, then pulled but it didn't budge. "It's locked too but…" He felt his fingers around the edges, "We might be able to pry it open… With something, maybe?" As he said it, he had no clue as to what they could use, *a crowbar would be great right now but?*

"Let me look at it", Mario said, water splashing as the big guy made his way, ducking under the wall. The sloshes were slow sounding as he tried to move with the pain.

"Be careful, your hurt", Marielle called out.

"I'll be fine, feeling better already!" He chimed clearly lying.

Marielle bit her lip as she and Leanne tried to peer into the hole to see, she heard her brother kick the door a few times, but he wasn't up to full strength yet.

"I need something to pry it, to put my weight on", He said sloshing back into the toilet block.

"Like what?" Marielle asked.

His big brown eyes scanned the room, looking for anything, something… then he looked haunted, and Marielle thought she knew what was coming. She shook her head, "No".

"Sis, it's grim, but it's the only thing that could be strong enough to hold my weight and pry the door open".

"What? What is?" Leanne said looking between them.

"The spike that impaled Nancy", Marielle replied.

"Oh, hell no", Leanne whined, "You can't be serious, that's sick".

"She would want us to get out, to survive", Mario said.

"Really? Would she? Would she want the spike pulled out of her brains?" Leanne's voice getting higher in pitch, almost hysterical.

"She wouldn't want us to give up", He protested.

"Why can't you just kick the door down!" She protested back.

"Why don't you go kick the door down!" He snapped back.

"Well, I can't I'm too small", she hissed.

"And I just got electrocuted!" He shouted.

"Your own fault I told you not to go that way", she said matter of factly.

Marielle could see her brothers blood boiling, "Look, Lee, Mario is hurt ok, he can't kick down the door, none of us can. This may be our only chance, our only choice".

"Well, I don't like it", she huffed.

"None of us do Lee, but sometimes in bad situations you have to do things you're not comfortable with", Marielle said trying to calm her down.

Leanne shrugged, "Fine, but I'm not watching".

"I didn't ask your permission Leanne, and I certainly didn't want to make a show out of it, I was going to go and get it anyway", Mario snapped and stormed off back the way they had come.

Before Leanne could say anything back to him, Marielle took her hand, Jared staying quiet in the corner. "I'm sorry Leanne, I know Nancy and you were really close".

"She was like a sister to me… Not that you cared".

"What?" Marielle said confused.

"Well, you stopped coming out with us, you got jealous of our friendship".

"I stopped seeing her so much for Mario", Marielle told her.

"Why?" Leanne said in a teasing tone.

"You know".

"Do I? Nancy told me that Mario wouldn't take no for an answer, that he would never leave her alone", Leanne smiled.

"Nothing ever happened between them", Marielle said.

"Only because Tristan walked in on them", she smirked.

"What are you talking about?"

"Mario tried it on with her, she said no, he wouldn't take no for an answer, but luckily me and Tristan were due to have a movie night with her... Tristan walked in, and he scarpered"

"No, you got it wrong, Nancy led Mario on, she did it for years to get him to do things for her!"

"Really? Like what?" Leanne's smug face glowing in the gloomy atmosphere.

"Beating people up that wronged her, buying her things when she ran out of money, he bailed her out of loads of debts that she racked up".

Leanne laughed, "Oh yeah, you remember that freaky girl at school, oh what was her name, Kayleigh-Ella or something? Didn't he beat her up for her?"

Marielle nodded, "Yeah... she um... got her grounded for something, I can't remember what but... Yeah, she got him to beat her up... You should remember that".

"So, he has form then? As a woman beater?"

Marielle felt her blood boil, but she heard Mario's footsteps coming back and decided to leave it be for now.

Death's Carousel

They had a bigger problem on their hands… But she would be having serious words with Leanne once they were out and free. Leanne had her skeletons in the closet, especially where it concerned the freaky girl at school… *Actually*, as she thought about it, *they all did*… But as quickly as the thought appeared it disappeared with Mario reappearing.

Mario appeared, his face sullen and sombre. He glanced at Marielle, his eyes saddened by what he just did. The pole gleamed in the weird light in the toilet block, but she could see he had wipe it somewhat clean of Nancy's blood and gore. He marched over to the hole in the wall, ducking under and heading right for the door. Marielle started to follow, as did Leanne. They were both nearly at the hole when Leanne slipped on something in the murky water. As she fell, she reached out, grabbing Marielle's hair and pulling her back and down with her.

Leanne managed to regain her footing before falling fully into the water, but Marielle fell straight in, the toxic wastewater stinging her nose as it was forced up there by the impact of her fall. The cold stinking water clung to her clothes as she broke the surface and gasped for air.

Leanne's face was full of instant disgust, "Oh my god I hate this place, get me out, get me out!" She looked down at her clothes that had bits of wastewater splashed over them. "I'm so fucking cold now".

Marielle felt anger boil under the surface, "Your cold? Are you actually fucking joking Lee?"

Leanne hissed at her, "You splashed me with shit water".

"I splashed you? You bloody pulled me over!"

Leanne rolled her eyes, "Oh give me a break, it's not as if your clothes are worth crying over, you look like crap anyway, might as well smell the part too".

"You bitch, what is your problem!"

"You! Nancy died, but your still here! That is my problem... She had my back but you. All you care about is you!"

Marielle felt dumbstruck, "You are kidding? All I care about is myself? Coming from you, the Queen of mean, all mighty bitch of bitch town... When was the last time you cared about me, or Nancy, or even Tristan for that matter huh? You care about him whilst your knobbing Jared?"

Shock filled Leanne's face, her normally pretty features turning an angry, an ugly shade of bitch and she lunged. She lunged at Marielle, her fingers outstretched like claws, swiping at Marielle's face. Stinging pain ripped across her cheek as she felt the scratch, her mind panicking at the thought of an open wound when her skin had been saturated by the stinking, grimy water. Leanne lunged again but this time Marielle was ready and slapped her friend across the face. Leanne recoiled in shock, her hand touching her cheek, but it lasted mere seconds, then she spun on her heel, lifting her leg and kicking out, her foot connecting with Marielle's chest. The air was knocked out of her, winded she fell once again into the cold putrid water. Leanne jumped, her whole-body weight slamming into her, her head slammed back into the water, it didn't cushion the blow and as she fell back hard her skull connected with the tiled floor underneath her with a loud sharp crack, but there was something else, something sharp… and numbness…

SMACK! SMACK! SMACK!

Leanne was then on top of her, punching and smacking her head, another crack to the floor as she lifted her out by the scruff of the neck and then thrashed her back down hard.

Marielle felt the world blur around her, her mind going numb, refusing to work, to fight. She knew Leanne played dirty when it came to fights or getting her own way, but Marielle had not expected this.

"Get off her".

Marielle suddenly felt lighter as the weight of Leanne was forced from her, she caught a glimpse of caramel hair flying through the air and the noise of a loud SPLASH! But then it was quiet, she felt dizzy, dark spots forcing their way into her eyesight… Then nothing…

*

Mario stabbed the pole between the door and the door frame and leant as hard as he could on it. His weight tilted the pole, forced it to move between structures of man-made substances. A splintering of wood told him it had worked and he pushed harder until the door flew open revealing a room with two doors beyond. Then he heard a commotion, Jared running back to check on the girls. It sounded like they were being murdered… *Had the killer snuck up on them… Taking out the girls whilst the guys were busy?*

Then he heard Jared shouting at Leanne to stop.

Mario ran, his footsteps pounding into the water, cool jets of liquid streamed up over him as his legs moved faster to get to Marielle. Ducking under the wall he was back in the room and saw Leanne on top of Marielle, her fist connecting with Marielle's face over, and over repeatedly. "Get off her!" he boomed and grabbed her hair, flinging her off and into the air. A loud splash signified her landing, but Mario was too concerned with his sister who was out cold and under the water, drowning!

He drove his arms under the murky depths and pulled his sister up and out the water. Her body limp, a dead weight. "No, No, No… Come on… This can't be happening".

Jared leaned forward to try and help but Mario batted his hand away. He grabbed her neck trying to feel for a pulse, but his fingers cold and numb, he couldn't feel one. Her chest wasn't moving, there was no rise and fall, she was gone… DEAD!

He turned, his eyes full of rage, "What have you done!". His voice boomed all around the room.

Leanne looked like a rabbit stuck in the glare of headlights, but then she moved, in a quick flash of movement and she was gone. She had ducked under the hole, run through the now open door and was gone.

Mario lay his sister down and raced after Leanne, back through the hole in the wall, grabbing the pole that he had dropped in the panic, "You better run bitch!" he screamed, "I will find you!"

*

Death's Carousel

Leanne scrambled under the wall, the panic and fear spurring her on faster. She slipped and fell into the cold water, but it wasn't as deep by the now open door. Pulling herself up she ran, ran through the door not caring or knowing what was ahead.

The door led to a smaller corridor that had two more doors, one to her left and one straight ahead. Coming to the first one on her left she tried the handle, it opened but in her blind panic she fumbled with the door and fell in. Heavy thumping footsteps sounded out behind her, she turned onto her back and kicked the door hard, it slammed shut and she heard the click of a lock sounding out. Seconds later Mario caught up and tried the handle, it spun but the door didn't budge. He kicked it in a fit of rage a few times, it rattled on its hinges but again didn't open.

Standing up she breathed a sigh of relief, until she inspected the door. Someone had fitted a dead bolt attached to a device that manually operated from elsewhere. Although it meant Mario couldn't reach her, it also meant she couldn't go back the way she came… She just hoped that meant she could escape and that the others were doomed instead of her.

Turning to look at the room she heard another door in the distance open and then close, *must have been the other door in the hall, must have been Mario*. She hoped that it didn't mean he would just turn up, but she had no way to know. All she could do was move.

*

"Mario! Mario! She's alive come back!" Jared shouted down the hallway where the hole in the wall led out to.

"Argh…cough", Marielle sounded out behind him, she sounded like death but at least she was alive.

"I don't think he can hear me, Marielle. Hopefully he will come back".

Her eyes fluttered, she was weak and judging by the red that had blossomed out around her in the water she had a severe head injury. She could be concussed alongside the injury, or worse.

Jared lifted her up, she cried out in pain, and she felt like a dead weight, "Can you move?" he asked, it would be so much easier for him to move her if she could aid in the task.

"No", she breathed, "Something…Something is wrong. I can't feel… my body".

He drew in all his strength and lifted her fully, adrenaline forced his weedy body to lift her. He was indeed no body builder or gym bunny, and he could feel his muscles tear from the exertion and strain on them. She wasn't a heavy girl in the slightest, but he was just not built for this. He struggled through the water, his feet threatening to slip but he held on, forcing his feet one footstep at a time, he didn't want to hurt her any more than she already was.

He spotted the sink area, although smashed around a bit, it was the only place in the room that he could lay her on and at least she would be out of the cold and rancid water. The sideboard that housed the sinks was still intact and hopefully strong enough to hold her weight. He lay her down and his stomach churned. A gaping hole in the back of her neck was exposed. When Leanne had thrown her down hard into the water it not only cracked her head but had impaled her on something sharp within the murky water. Oozing thick blood gushed out from the wound, no wonder she felt so bad, she was probably paralysed from the wound in her neck, maybe it had penetrated her spinal cord or… Jared shook his head, he was no doctor, in fact, he wasn't even much of an Estate Agent either.

He trailed his hand through his damp hair, looking around for something to help, maybe a first aid kit, or something. He had watched enough films and TV to know that the wound needed pressure and something on it to stem the bleeding, but that with her neck wound and him moving her he may have done more damage. But she couldn't stay on the floor in the water, it was cold and full of germs.

CLICK!

The cleaner's cupboard door was swinging open on its own. Probably whoever was doing this had pushed a button to reveal what was behind door number 1!

Jared made his way to it, hopefully there was a first aid kit, a phone or anything. He ignored the feeling that came over him. *Someone had opened that door remotely, just for him, and that made him uneasy. What was he going to find in there?*

He approached cautiously and watched out for any sharp objects, or electrical hums that may be waiting to get him. But all he could see was a porta-loo, randomly built into the cupboard… *But why?* The Porta-loo, the type of toilet people rented out when they had no other means of a bathroom, like a concert, festival, building sites etc… *But why was it here in a toilet block? So, strange...* Leaning in he rummaged around, there was a few boxes and empty bottles of bleach lining the floor but all of them... Empty.

Defeated he walked back over to Marielle, her chest rising and falling in shallow breaths. Her eyes closed but they fluttered as he approached.

"I need to stem the bleeding on your neck", he said taking off his top and gently lifting her head. He bunched it into a makeshift ball and the guided it to where the wound was.

She grimaced in pain, a soft cry breaking out from between her dry and now crusted lips.

He shivered in the chill of the room, "What now?" he asked himself.

*

Marielle hissed as the pain rifled through her skull and down her body. After a few moments it subsided, but she still couldn't feel much else. She knew deep inside something was wrong with her, really, really wrong... But she didn't want to accept it. She kept trying to move an arm, a finger, a toe, but nothing done as she asked. The only thing she could control was her face and even that hurt like hell to do.

She could hear Jared muttering to himself, sploshing around as he searched the room, waiting for Leanne or Mario to make a re-appearance.

CLICK!

Death's Carousel

Another click had sounded out before opening the closet door, but this click sounded different, like a needle being placed on a record... Then the song began...

"Porta-loo-ooooooo, Porta-loo-ooooooo".

She had to stifle a giggle, *a song about a toilet. Was this chick ok in the head?* She heard Jared stop what he was doing and look inquisitively up to where a speaker was positioned.

"You messaged me a playdate, so I came to your home, there's others there that came to play, but they leave me alone... You tell them 'oh the poor Freak' she just wants to play, but truly, really, I don't want to stay".

The words seemed silly, confusing somehow, a toilet and a playdate? How did the two connect?

"Your playin, playin spin the bottle, Let's go full throttle, on the freakazoid... Ah, Ah... Loo... She's a freak so, she has no feeling, spin it to the ceiling, to the porta-loo".

Spin the bottle? Porta-loos? This girl is crazy... Yet... A distant memory wanted to surface, something familiar and knowing about those words. That voice too... It sounded familiar, like someone she knew...

"You don't give a shit about our friendship now, you'd rather be plastic like your loo, you grab my head and push me down, you flush the water of the porta-loo".

Tears fell down Marielle's cheeks, she tried to blink them back, to stop them falling but it was no use.

"Hey...Hey don't cry", Jared said rushing over, "It will be fine... It will be ok, we will get you help and..."

She cut him off, "I know who's doing this to us..."

His face paled, "You do?"

She wanted to nod but she couldn't, so she simply whispered, "Yes".

"Who?" He asked confused.

"A girl... a girl from school that we all picked on. I know what I did, I know what Nancy did... I know what Leanne did to her...This is her revenge... She's killing us but using what we did to her as our death", she breathed out the words, it sounded so unreal, made up, like a story of some mad killer... But it was true... she could feel it, she knew it had to be her.

Jared looked shocked but a look of realisation came over his face, "I think I know the girl... I... I didn't really know her but... Leanne she..."

Marielle knew Leanne had to be the one to have got Jared involved with this. He had been a newer member to their friendship group and hadn't been around for their 'bullying' days as much but... *Maybe recently? Or had he been around enough to do things to her too?* She couldn't pull her thoughts together enough to remember it all.

"Kayella?" he asked.

"Yes", she replied bluntly, "But what did you do?"

He sighed and again ran his fingers through his messy, damp blond hair, it had curled in the dampness, giving him a young, surfer guy look, "Leanne she... Me and her we have been, seeing each other". He looked over at Marielle and she had a knowing look in her eyes, "I know it was wrong, she and Tristan were... are, engaged to be married but... We've been sleeping together for years. She had a plan", He paused taking a deep breath, "Tristans dad, his family treated me like a son, when my dad divorced my mum and left us, he took me under his wing.

Death's Carousel

Everything him and Tristan did together they included me. When Tristan decided that he wanted to pursue a career in computer science and engineering his dad approached me and asked if I wanted to be trained as an Estate Agent in his company. He trained me up, paid me well, I got promoted to senior sales manager with a big bonus and… Well Leanne… She came up with a plan".

There was a moments silence between them but then he continued, "If she married Tristan and bought a house with him, then after a year or so she could divorce him and take half or more. Then with my money from the business and her half we could buy one of the biggest houses in town. All she cared about was showing off, and showing everyone what she has or had… Well not yet she doesn't but… Kayella came into the shop, she'd come into money, come of age to receive it or something, when her mum had passed or her nan, I can't quite remember but she'd been left a substantial amount, a good amount to put a deposit down on a little house on the outskirts of town. Leanne had told me if she ever came in that I was to refuse, and I was to… phone my friend at the bank and get them to refuse a mortgage if I couldn't stop her at my end. So, I did… And I was mean about it too".

"So, you stopped her buying a house?" Marielle asked, "Because Leanne told you to? Was there anything else you did to her?"

He nodded, "Yeah Leanne told me to, I mean I can't totally blame her can I. I didn't have to do it, and I actually enjoyed seeing the look on the girls face especially when the house of her dreams sold to someone else… But Leanne can be, very persuasive too! She told me she would rat me out to Tristan and his dad, tell them that I wouldn't leave her alone, that I was pursuing her against her will and that she would ruin me… So, I guess I kind of had no choice. I love Tristan, he's like my brother… And it would've been hard enough to eventually tell him about me and Leanne once they divorced but… at least I could have maybe still had my 'Brother'…" He trailed off.

"Are you sure there was nothing else you did to her? Something else she could use against you?" Marielle just had a feeling that the house thing wouldn't be it, Kayella was attacking them with the physical things they had done to her, but preventing a house purchase… Yeah it was crappy, *but was it murderous enough?*

"No, no I don't…think so…" He replied but he looked unsure, "Maybe… But I can't remember. I know me and Lee hung out down the town a lot we picked on a few kids every so often, but I can't remember if it was her or not".

"I think you should take it that you did, you did something else to her", Marielle replied, she was feeling weaker and weaker by the minute, she felt horrendously drained and although she couldn't feel her body to move it, she could feel the cold, the damp and the ache.

"What did you do? To Kayella?" He asked.

It was Marielle's turn to sigh, she didn't want to tell him, to be shown up as the awful person she had been. Since hitting her twenties, she had tried really hard to try and be a better person, to treat others how she would want to be treated but… The damage she guessed had already been done… Especially to Kayella!

Death's Carousel

"I used to be friends with Kayella, me and Nancy, we both did. We were a little threesome, but the bullying got so bad from Leanne towards her that Leanne would often turn on us", She bit her lip to try and stop her voice from cracking, "Poor Kayella, she… She came from a poor family. Her mum lost the plot and… well…" She shrugged, "You know… And her dad, well Kayella was a girl not a boy, so he abandoned her. Left her with the nan, the nan who was old, frail, poor and clearly had dementia, she would remember certain things about Kayella, like her singing lessons, and helping her use the sewing machine… But then she would forget other things like, food, to pay the heating bill so they got cut off, so they only had cold water to wash in and… Everyone knew it, but everyone was just so mean to her over it. Especially us…"

She stopped to take a breath, her skull pounding but she needed to say it out loud, to tell him her story, to get it off her chest, to tell all her sins, to repent before death finally took her. She wanted, needed, craved some form of forgiveness and redemption.

"But why the porta-loo? Why this place? Why the carousel for Nancy?" Jared asked.

"This place was where we spent a lot of our summers and was a place that we dished out a lot of our pranks on Kayella. Nancy, she tied Kayella to the Carousel and force fed her rotten food to make her sick… hence the Carousel death for Nancy… For me… We were having work done at our house, our bathroom refitted… we had a rented porta-loo in the garden, just for a week but me, Nancy and Leanne had the cruel idea to get Kayella round for a playdate, a girly day… but… it was a ruse to lure her to the toilet and we, well I… Flushed her head down the toilet. The weird blue chemical that is in the toilet to keep it kind of sanitary burnt her skin, she was allergic to some ingredient or chemical in it. She spent weeks in hospital. Then when she came out, she was scarred in places and extra sensitive to the sun, every time she went out, summer or winter, she had to wear sunscreen or risk being burnt again".

Jared looked shocked, horrified, "You did that to her?"

"Yes, I'm not proud of it and it wasn't until afterwards that I realised the risks… We could have blinded her, I could have blinded her…"

"Man, that was nasty… I know I was mean but…Wait? Do you think she will kill me? How will she do it? Death by money? Death by Estate Agent?" he laughed, trying to bring in a little humour to the situation.

Marielle let out a small laugh, "Maybe or death by house". The laugh caused her to cough, and she tasted iron, she felt liquid dribble down her crusted lips and down her chin.

Jared looked alarmed and wiped her mouth with his hand, "Shit, we need to get you to a hospital. And the others aren't back", he looked around again, seeing the small slit of a window. He climbed up bashing on the glass, but he knew it was pointless, he wouldn't fit, and Marielle was in no shape to move.

"Jared stop! It's fine… I've accepted my fate".

He looked at her, "No, no I will get help".

The music began to play around them again, the next verse coming through… "Porta-loo-oooooooo, Porta-loo-oooooooo, Coughing, choking, poison, burning in my lungs, trying to breathe, this shit water isn't fun… When I try to talk to you my words don't make a hit, this playdate … is burning like hells pit… this playdate is so frickin boring, now that you are whoring, in your porta-loo…!"

The words Kayella sung were sung with such heartache, anger and the need for revenge that Marielle could feel herself willing it to be, to happen already, so she could repent for her sins and apologise in the afterlife for the pain she had inflicted on the girl.

"Your playin, playin spin the bottle, let's go full throttle on the freakazoid… Porta-loo-oooooooo… She's a freak, so she has no feeling, spin it to the ceiling, to the porta-loo-oooooooo".

"What about the others?" Jared asked, "What did they do to her?"

Marielle tried to speak but she couldn't, theirs wasn't her story to tell. Nancy couldn't speak for herself anymore, so she needed someone to know her story… But the others, they could tell him once she was gone. Plus, with Leanne there were many things she had done to Kayella. Kayella could choose to murder her in many different ways.

"Marielle?" He pushed. But he could see that her body was weakening, her eyes trying to close but she was forcing them open with whatever might and strength she had left inside her.

"You don't give a shit about our friendship now, you'd rather be plastic like your loo, you grab my head and push me down, you flush the water of the porta-loo".

Piper Nuelle

*

Leanne was running again, she'd left the first room behind, it was what looked like a supply room for what could be a play zone and a kid friendly cafeteria. Boxes of plastic play pit balls, boxes of sauces and condiment packets, all congealed and rotten, packets of plastic cutlery, knives, forks, spoons, cups… But nothing to help defend herself, or to eat or drink. Her body began to shake and ache with a need for food or water.

Her heart pounded loudly in her chest and all she could hear was the blood rushing to her ears, almost blocking out any other sound around her. She was good at blocking things out, blocking out the whinging and whining of the people she was training to help, she only went the therapist route for the money, not to help others, she couldn't give a rat's ass about little *'Johnny'* and his past traumas, all she wanted was the pay cheque that talking to these traumatised people would give.

She came to a stop at yet another door, she paused for a moment catching her breath before she gingerly opened it. She opened it slowly, trying to hold in any sound it may make, she didn't want Mario or the crazed killer to hear and ultimately find her. Seen as both wanted to kill her, she had to be extra careful.

As she had suspected from the storage supplies in the other room, she had come to a kiddie play zone. A very dank, dark and depressing one, but none the least it was a play area. The large, netted area that housed the fun house with the plastic balls and soft colourful play mats was lit up by some broken florescent lighting strips. It gave the area a spooky eerie glow. A deflating bouncy castle was to one end of the room, to the other end was a café area complete with grimy plastic tables and chairs. She noted another door that said toilets, and she paused, holding her breathe. If Mario was still looking for her, it would be that door he would burst through.

Feeling herself spiral she noted that the café area had a serving hatch that was unlocked, if danger presented itself, she could always run and hide in there, but first she needed to rest. She wasn't used to running so much, and the effects of being potentially drugged, hungry and thirsty and planted in some hellhole her by the killer had left her body weakened and tired. She took a seat on one of the crappy plastic chairs and looked around the room.

She took off her shoes and began to rub her aching damp feet, when something caught her eye. A liquid, glistening in the eerie lighting. Putting her shoes back on she tried peering out at it, but she was too far away, she needed to go closer.

Standing up and swallowing her fear she decided to check it out. Her footsteps seemed to echo loudly on the plastic flooring, but she didn't seem to notice or care, especially since the liquid had made her heart go in her throat.

The liquid was red, blood red, but washed out, watered down. But laying inside the liquid, just to the side of a strange, netted bridge that had connected the deflated castle to the netted play area was a body, a body she recognised.

She went to go to her, to her friend but heard the telltale buzz of electricity, the same buzz that had zapped

Mario not too long ago. The netted bridge had wires hanging from it, connected once again to car batteries.

She gasped at the horror before her, of what had happened to Sinead, her friend.

Sinead lay there, frozen in a state of watery, electrified death. Her shoes lay to one side of her, her favourite designer brand.

Leanne couldn't keep it in, she turned and threw up all over the floor beneath her feet. The sight of another death rocking her whole body with shock, anger and rage. Tears rolled down her cheeks again, her eyes puffing up as she sobbed sad, wracked sobs.

"Why? Why is this happening to us... To me?" She whispered into the gloom, but no one replied, not even Sinead.

Sinead had been a good friend, and a loyal push over. She did what ever Leanne said, and it had made them close. Maybe even closer than her and Nancy. Although she knew Nancy had fancied her and that was why she kissed the ground she walked on, but Sinead... Sinead was different. She didn't kiss ass for affection and or love, oh no! Leanne loved Sinead for her ruthlessness, her desire to be at the top, to get where and what she wanted. And the fact that they both would do whatever it took to get to where they wanted, climbing and stepping on whoever was in their way, well that made Leanne appreciate Sinead even more. They were besties, soul mates... Partners in crime.

Once empty and no longer able to shed another tear she turned to head to the serving hatch, she needed a way out, this place was fucked. She had no idea that Sinead was here, she had just presumed it had been herself, Jared,

Nancy, Mario and Marielle. But this changed things, this meant that more of them could be here, more of their group, waiting, hurting, dying… But maybe they were alive, which meant they could help to keep her safe, they could get her out alive…

She lifted the hatch to the kitchen and held it in place whilst she scanned the area. Nothing moved or jumped out at her, no Mario waiting to bash her brains in, no serial killer with a mask and a knife and no rats. Hooking the hatch up she hoisted herself up and over and thudded to the tiled kitchen floor.

Pots, pans, old rotten food that had turned to mulchy dust decorated the floor and the sides. An old dishwasher sat half loaded, black mould and slime slithered out from it. A small boxy window sat way high up above the cupboards, but it looked to be boarded up from the outside as no moonlight slivered in, just more gloom and doom from the pitch-black darkness.

She took a few steps in, her shoe hitting an empty tin can that rolled in the gloom and made a deafening rattle as it hit another tin. She held her breath waiting for footsteps or noise, but nothing came. *Maybe Mario had given up? Maybe Marielle was alright, and he was just overreacting? Maybe?*

She made it to the other end of the kitchen, nearly tripping over a mop and bucket filled with brown water as she placed her hand over the handle of another door. Dead flies floated along the surface, a milky, soapy substance making a film that prevented them from sinking down to the bottom. She gently shifted the grubby bucket across the floor to make more room for her, she didn't want to come face to face with Mario and stumble back into mop sludge. As she moved it the flies bobbed along the top of a ripple of water, almost like they were dancing, dancing to a music she could just about hear… She placed her ear against the door and listened, she could hear singing, that sweet and soft female voice calling out like a siren in the night. Then she heard a mechanical chain rattling, it sounded like it was in the wall.

"Come on you fucker! Take me… ARGHHHH!" She heard the furious cry of Mario behind the door, she was about to turn and run when she heard the gurgle of his cries, they changed, sounded wet and… BANG… then Silence.

She stood there, frozen to the spot for a few moments, then the door she leant on clicked open, it fell inwards with her weight on it, and she fell flailing to the floor. She threw her hands up in defence, waiting for Mario to do something to her, but nothing…

She opened her eyes and looked around the new room, the ceiling looked, odd. A large platform hovered on chains, but what struck her as really weird was the large cut out holes, there was about nine of them, quite large, large enough for a man to stand in when the ceiling was lowered, but what struck her as equally weird was the random droplets of rain, blood red rain that dripped from one of the holes in the ceiling.

Gulping down her fear she leant over to peer fully into the hole, above it was a large wooden like hammer, blood and brain matter clung to it, dripping off from it in thick sludges of gore, splatting meat onto the ceiling and down through the hole.

Death's Carousel

Confusion spread through her, then she spotted the source of the gore ridden hammer… Mario!

Her brain couldn't make sense of his face, it had been pulverised, smashed to a bloody pulp. His body sat back on a chair, his legs splayed open in an awkward dead position, his arms limp at his side, the golden gilded pole that had impaled Nancy lay by his side on the floor. His top was covered in chunks of his face, teeth and chips of skull littered the front of him and the floor beside him.

She began to hyperventilate, two dead bodies in as many minutes, but now three of her friends dead… Anxiety filled her body, a panic attacked clung at her lungs, making it hard to breathe, hard to move. She threw her hand up to clutch at her chest.

And when the doorway filled with a presence of some dark hooded figure she felt like crying, fear dripping into her eyes, she held up her hands in a surrender, only to have what looked like a 'Whack a mole' hammer crack against her skull and she dropped to the floor like a sack of shit.

*

"Flush it down, flush it down, you flush it so I cannot scream, flush it down, flush it down, you're going to fall apart at the seams".

Jared stood by Marielle's side, the song must be nearing its climax which meant surely Kayella would want her dead, even if she was already halfway there. *But surely, she couldn't have planned for Leanne and her to scuffle, to fight, to nearly kill one another… Could she?*

He stood staring at the porta-loo, he wondered, *what it was that Kayella wanted to do? But all he knew was that if she tried to come in here and kill Marielle, he would attack her first and make it all stop.*

"You don't give a shit about our friendship now, you'd rather be plastic like your loo, you grab my head and push me down, you flush the water of the porta-loo…"

A hiss of static filled the room which made Jared jump out of his skin, he glared up at the speaker which crackled before Kayella spoke, softly and sweetly to him.

"I have a special request for you Jared, if you do it, I may let you live…"

Jared shook his head, dismayed that she thought he would be stupid enough to fall for that, "You're still going to kill me no matter what… You won't let me live, I know who you are, your motivations".

A girly giggled echoed out all around him, threatening to rot his teeth with the sweetness that poured out, "Hmmmm, maybe you do? Maybe you don't? But maybe it's not just my motivations that you need to be scared of…" She trailed of then swiftly added, "My request is you are going to flush Marielle's head down the Porta-loo toilet… Until she breathes no more".

He shook his head, "No, no way", he looked down at the pitiful woman that lay before him, her mouth crusted with dry blood, murky water stains all over her clothes, the fluttering of her eyes trying to stay awake, trying to stay alive, "She's my friend", he added.

"Hmmmm, friend seems a strong word… Would you not consider her a frenemy?", Kayella sang over the speaker, so much humour and glee in her voice.

Death's Carousel

"No, why frenemy?" He asked confused.

"I would say ask her, but I don't think she's in any fit state to talk really, is she? Might be best just to put her out of her misery", Kayella said and then carried on, "But... She knew of you and Leanne... She knew of Leanne's adulterous ways, cheating on her soon to be husband... She might have accidentally let slip, she might have known about how you two planned to screw over a lovely, decent family that took you in, gave you a job, treated you like a son... All for money..."

Jared felt his blood run cold, "No, she didn't know, I only told her moments ago. Your lying, you just listened in and are recycling it against me".

"Ok... but why are you here?" She asked him.

"I... I refused to sell you a house, I told the mortgage advisor to refuse you a mortgage... I..."

"True, I agree you did that to me, but... the people that are here have wronged me in huge ways as a child, as a teenager... You and I had one maybe two interactions... How would I kill you? Like you said, death by house maybe? Or was there something else?"

He shifted uneasily on his feet, looking between the speaker and then to Marielle.

"How are you and Tristan now a days?" She asked, that evil sense of humour pouring into the room.

He gulped a breath down, "Ok".

"You sure about that?" She asked.

He looked at Marielle, her eyes flickering but a pain and sadness swallowed up by the rest of her face.

There was a moment of silence, and he wondered if she had left the room, left the mic… But then a voice sounded that wasn't hers.

"Hello Jared", it was Tristan's voice echoing around the gloomy wet room.

Jared's heart sank, Tristan knew, of course he knew, "Tristan mate, brother… I"

"Save your apologies", Tristan snapped.

Jared sank into himself.

"Marielle told me it all Jared, Leanne confided in her when drunk a couple of months ago and I had to keep my cool, pretend everything was fine… Then I bumped into Kayella, she told me what you did at my family's estate agents, and I knew, you thought you had more power than you should have. But this has been going on and off for years you and Lee, right? Since, prom night? My dad had already promised you my job because I didn't want it, and good money, Leanne knew I too would earn good money once qualified and then with my own business. And now you two planning to screw over my dad's hard-earned company and then for her to marry me and take half in the divorce!" Tristan paused, but Jared could feel the anger in the room, it emitted out like a beacon. "The only reason you are here is because of Marielle, if she hadn't of spilt the tea on you and Lee, I wouldn't have been none the wiser… Marielle has put you in this position, signed your death certificate for you".

Jared starred down at Marielle, a well of hatred and anger growing inside him. He knew it was wrong, he knew it was his fault, him and Leanne caused this for each other… But Marielle, exposing them and now they were all dying because of it. No, no… The others died for what they did to Kayella, *I didn't do anything to her… Maybe… Or did I?* The fear was blocking the memory that was trying to surface.

"If I do it…Kill Marielle, will you let me go?" He asked, "I know Kayella is murdering the others because of the nasty things they did to her… But… I didn't do anything to her, well, not like them. I know I've hurt you, broken your trust, but we are like brothers, right?" His voice sounded hopeful, begging and feigning some form of innocence, like a true coward, like the coward he truly was.

"We were brothers yes", Tristan agreed, "But show me now… What will my brother do for me now to make things better?"

Jared looked down at Marielle, she was pretty much already dead, it would be kinder to put her out of her misery, "What about Leanne?" He had to ask.

Tristan didn't answer right away, instead it seemed he was contemplating his choice of words, "Leanne's fate is out of my hands".

Jared felt a wave of sadness hit him, a lone tear fell down his cheek, "Kayella is going to kill her?"

"Yes", Tristan replied, "I cannot change that, but I can change your fate".

Jared ran his hands through his hair, a nervous motion, a million things racing through his mind. "How do I know you will keep to your word?"

"You don't, you just have to hope my word is better than yours".

"And if you do keep me alive, what will happen then? I will know who you are, what you both did, how can you trust I won't grass you up?" Jared said.

"We won't, but we are both dangerous, especially… Kayella. She will find a way to shut you up one way or another".

"I, I won't do it", he gasped, his voice cracking under the strain.

"Yes, you will", Kayella joined in.

"No, I won't. Why don't you come in and do it yourself".

Silence… And then CLICK!

A secret hidden panel moved from behind one of the old flooded, overflowing toilets. Beady eyes peered out from behind the pipe work that had been built like a cage, a squeak, and another and another… Then in flooded a dark mass of slimy fur. The water rippled from their movement, like a tiny flood of infectious terror.

"They are hungry Jared", Kayella said sweetly.

Bile rose in his gullet, *he hated, no despised rats! Because of her!* He had a phobia of them, their beady eyes, long worm like tails and germ ridden mouths… He could feel his heart rate quicken with the panic. One reached his ankle and tried to climb up his leg, it squeaked loudly as he shook it off, it fell, sloshing back into the dank water, but it didn't matter as another one had lunged, jumped up climbed on his leg and nipped him.

He cried out in fear, "I'll do it, I'll do it… Just get me out of here!"

"Very well", Kayella mused, "Take her head and flush it, once she stops breathing, we will let you out".

Death's Carousel

He felt disgusted at himself for what he was about to do, but he kept telling himself she was already dead, he was being cruel to be kind. He lifted her up, her limp body a dead weight against his chest. She let out a frail moan from her throat in protest, but whether it was from her trying to stop him or in pain he would never know. He carried her over to the porta-loo, the grimy off blue plastic shone with a deathly glow.

His lip trembled, tears poured down his cheeks, anger flooded through him as he held Marielle down into the bowl of the toilet and pulled the chain, pulled the flush… Anger at Marielle for spilling the beans, anger at Kayella for coming up with this sick fun fair of terror, Tristan for not waiting, not waiting for him and Leanne to live out their plan, he had made it so that one day he and Tristan could have still been like brothers, just made it out to be a simple mistake, a broken heart after a divorce… He was angry at Leanne for tormenting Kayella the way she had, then maybe the girl wouldn't have gone full psycho on them, and no one would be dead or dying, but ultimately, he was angry at himself. Angry for treating his brother like this, for treating his family like this, and for treating Kayella like he had that fateful day in the Estate Agents!

He could see it, the full conversation…

*   *   *

The door to Hinchcliff and Co Estate Agents opened, the small old-fashioned bell that hung above the door chimed as a rather strangely beautiful woman walked in. She had curves in all the right places, her dark glossy long hair was tied back into a high ponytail, her makeup was of professional level, she wore shades over her eyes, and she exuded money.

    Jared rose from his desk at the back of the shop, the other desks were empty as it had been a slow week and nearing closing time and being the only Estate Agents in their small town was at times tiring. There were only so many homes to sell and rent out at a time, but the Air B n B business was beginning to boom, which was a saving grace as many property owners in the town had decided to expand or build on to their homes to make way for the sudden rush of tourism in the area. Not many small towns now were still mostly untouched and picturesque, but Rivervalle was one of the few. The only eyesore was the abandoned fairground down at Riverside, but word had it that the town was going to force the grounds to be sold, which would mean some sort of development would happen. Maybe some apartments, a few new house builds, or maybe even some shops, although in this economic climate shops were closing down quicker than being opened. But Jared was waiting for the day the planning and development began, *being the only Estate Agents in town would of course mean payday for him, for them…* KACHING!

    The bell above the door chimed again, taking him out of his thoughts, but the door didn't open or close again. The woman just stood there waiting. *Maybe the wind?*

    He made his way over to the stunning woman, and as she removed her shades, he recognised her immediately. Kayella!

Death's Carousel

Her dark eyes were bright, full of laughter, and an unsettling calmness too, almost too calm. Not the Kayella he remembered from school or from what Leanne had told him about her, "Hi", she beamed looking around the shop, "Just you?"

He nodded, "Yeah, just me. How can I help you today?" he let her know he recognised her but chose not to say her name.

"If you ever get that BITCH, come into your shop, you refuse her a house, you understand me? Rented or bought… She deserves nothing!" Leanne's face flashed before him and her words echoed loudly in his mind. He motioned for Kayella to sit down at his desk.

"I want to buy a house", she replied.

He sat back down, running his hands through his hair, "Oh, well you need money to do that", he exclaimed.

She narrowed her eyes, but they still lit up, in fact, they seemed to be more amused. The look made him feel uncomfortable.

"Oh yeah I forgot about that, damn it…" she grabbed her purse and opened up her phone, she selected her banking app and brought up her savings fund account. "Oh, I think this will be enough for a deposit on the house I've seen".

He glanced at the phone and sure enough she had a nice, tidy lump sum of money, more than enough for a reasonable deposit. Licking his lips he said, "What is the house you are enquiring about?"

She again went for her purse and pulled out a sheet of paper and passed it to him. It was a brochure print out of a house they were selling online via their website. It was a sweet little house, more like a little cottage, surrounded by a dainty brick wall covered in Ivy. A more 'British style' cottage home, he knew the house and the area very well, just off Riverpoint Lane. Clearly Miss Kayella wanted to live the quiet life hidden on the outskirts of town, away from all the hustle and bustle.

"Ahh, I'm afraid it's sold", he lied.

She frowned, no lines furrowed in her forehead though, she'd clearly had Botox and or other surgeries done. *Shame, she had always been naturally pretty*, he thought.

"And anyway, I don't think the bank will give you a mortgage", he added.

She stared at him, those sparkling dark eyes pouring into his very soul, searching him from the inside out. "And why don't you think the bank will give me the mortgage?"

He licked his lips again, his mouth feeling very dry, like someone had stuffed a cotton pad in there, "Well, Leanne and I are very friendly with the mortgage advisor there and well… A quick phone call and I know they will deny you".

"Why? Why would you do that?" she asked.

He shrugged, "No one likes you, Kayella. I'm sorry it's just the way it is".

"Just the way it is?" She mused.

"Look can you leave, you're making me feel uncomfortable", he stated starting to stand up from his desk to lead her out.

"Oh, I'm making you feel uncomfortable?" she said, "I am so sorry about that". She smiled, two rows of perfectly set white film star teeth grinned out at him. Her plump lips smiling with her delicate features.

She stood up to leave and reached the door, "Oh Jared, before I forget."

"Hmm…" He tried to look unbothered.

"You will regret this", she smiled and then turned on her heel and left. The bell chime on the door jingled with the motion of her departure, but it almost felt like the tone had changed, the pitch of the bell had dulled.

TH-DUNK… The bell fell off of its hinges and clattered noisily to the floor, broken.

Jared let out a breath he had been holding, grabbing his keys he headed to the door and locked up the shop, he would deal with the mess tomorrow. He felt unnerved and just wanted to go home, Kayella's presence was… Unsettling, something about her was different and not just her appearance.

Peering out into the parking lot where the shop was situated along the main high street of the town, he saw Kayella sitting in her car. It was a brand-new Honda Civic Type R, a white one with black wheels and red brake callipers peeking out. She definitely had come into money, and she could have afforded that house, but he'd rather the wrath of the freaky girl over the wrath of Leanne.

Rain had begun to fall, making the high street look gloomy and dank. A sense of unease shivered through him as she drove away slowly, waving to him as she passed the shop.

He headed out to the back door to the staff car park, his car sitting alone tucked away under a tree. Something looked odd about the tree, its wisping branches reaching out like cold evil hands and they were holding something. He reached up to the branch above his car and pulled down what looked like a doll of some sort. It had a zipper in the back, he pulled it open to see a tube of super glue and something else... something slim, fleshy pink and grey in colour and long... A tail. He shuddered and threw the tail on the floor. It had to be a Rat's tail!

Puzzled he looked around the car park. *Had it been Kayella?* But she hadn't come this way, she had come in and out the front of the shop and then driven away. *Or had she placed it before coming into the shop? But how would she know he would refuse her?*

Climbing in his car he shut the door and locked it from the inside. His nerves getting the better of him, making his breathing shallow and restless. *Why glue? Why the tail? Was she calling him a Rat?* Then it hit him... He hadn't bothered much with the bullying Kayella at school, not like the others. He had been more, distant, preferred to just hang with Tristan and play football, but there had been that one time. It had been a cruel joke on his part, he had been with Leanne, Marielle, Nancy and Mario, they had been hanging out at the local arcade which sat opposite the main supermarket in their small but bustling town. Leanne had spotted Kayella walking up, a shopping list in hand.

Being the vain princess she was, she had a tube of nail glue in her handbag for press on nail mishaps and she had quickly passed it to Jared, egging him on.

He'd rushed over to the supermarket and grabbed a trolley, smearing the nail glue all over the handle. As Kayella approached, he made sure to hold the side handles and pretended to be helping her out. He presented her the trolley and waited for her hands to clamp round the handle, she had even said thanks, a cute little smile, a brief moment of happiness of someone being nice to her until... She realised! He clamped his hands down over hers so she couldn't lift them off quick enough. Moments later and they were stuck fast.

She had cried out in horror as her hands stuck to the handle, tears rolling down her cheeks. For a moment Jared felt bad, felt sick to his stomach at the grief and horror that had filled her eyes. But then Leanne was beside him, laughing, cheering him on, congratulating him for this win against the freak.

They had all done a runner when the stores security guard came out to investigate.

He'd later heard from Tristan's mum when she went to get her nails filled in that the Nail technician from a few shops down had to come down with acetone to melt the glue and prise her poor hands from the handles.

He'd felt mean, but at the same time, invigorated, plus it had brought him and Leanne closer.

He shook his head at the memory, and it whooshed away, almost whooshed as much as the rain that began to pelt and hammer down heavily on the car. The noise was so loud that he didn't hear the subtle squeaks behind him, subtle ones that began to grow angry. When he realised that the squeaks were inside the car it was too late, a huge rat ran under his seat into the footwell of his car.

He let out a scream and began stamping his feet, smashing hard onto the pedals, until one of the pedals wouldn't go down anymore, the rat had hidden underneath it... SPLAT! He thundered his foot down hard onto the pedal and crushed the rodent underneath. Blood splattered over the footwell, his shoes and all over the pedals. His foot slipping off as he lifted it up.

"Oh man", he moaned in disgust.

How the hell had a Rat got into his locked car?

*   *   *

Jared came back into the room from the memory that ripped through his core. He felt Marielle give out a couple of shuddering movements, but her weak body couldn't fight back. Then as quick as he came round and pulled his hand away in disgust at what he had been coerced into doing she was gone. Her dead, limp body hanging over the bowl.

"No, no...Shit. What have I done", he grasped Marielle's shoulders and pulled her down to the floor. The blue liquid from the Porta-loo ran out from her nose and mouth, her dead eyes glassed over, looking but not looking at him.

He placed his hands on her chest and attempted CPR, he went to breathe into her mouth when he began to feel dizzy. Not sick dizzy from what he had done, but like, something was wrong dizzy.

He glanced at the Porta-loo, saw the blue liquid, but he could now smell bleach and maybe some other cleaning agent. He thought back to the flush, the flush of the toilet, the mixture of chemicals all merging together as one, intertwining, creating... *Mustard gas!*

He fell, slumping over Marielle's dead form, he struggled to breath, the mixture of chemicals burning his lungs and making him fall unconscious. The rats that had come surging in before where now retreating from the toxic smell, a few faltered and collapsed at Jared's feet, but the rest fled out the way they had come in.

His last thought before falling asleep was how this wasn't the end, he knew Kayella had something else in store for him. He would die by her hand, they had both lied to him, they had got him to do their dirty work and now he would pay for it all…

How had he forgotten what he had done to her?

*

Marielle died inside as Jared lifted her up and walked over to the Porta-loo. Kayella had done her homework, not only was she punishing them all for what they had done to her, how they tortured her as a child and into her teens, but she had found ways to turn them against one another. She was ultimately the murderer, but now they were killing one another on her behalf. *How had they underestimated the girl so bad?* And roping Tristan in to help her, making him mad by what Leanne and Jared had done or were going to do to him and his family… *Genius*.

Tristan had always had a soft spot for Kayella, if Leanne hadn't of dug her claws in deep Marielle reckoned that those two would have been together instead. *Maybe Kayella would have been happy? Maybe she would have healed and not felt the need for revenge, or at least not in such a deadly way.*

Although Marielle was scared of the impending death that was fast approaching, she knew that what they had done to that poor girl had clearly given her mental health issues, that they had turned her into this monster, and that in reality, this was all their Karma! She chuckled inside at the thought that Leanne would finally get her comeuppance and as Jared lifted her head into the toilet bowl, she fully accepted her fate and let it go.

The musical songstress started up the chords once again, and Marielle could feel the violence in the air, it felt thick and strong… *Or was that something else she could sense?*

"I don't give a shit about our friendship now, I'm gonna be plastic just like you…"

Jared pushed her head down and pulled the chain, the strong blue chemicals flooded down the bowl. It splashed all up her face, in her ears, in her mouth, up her nose. The taste was rancid, a strong bleachy taste mixed with crap. Her brain tried to kick in, to stop her from drowning, self-preservation trying and failing. She overwrote the programming in her brain and opened her mouth, breathing in the thick chemicals, they burnt as they travelled down her throat into her lungs. She felt her body fight back, but she felt so weak and worn out, that within seconds her body began to shut down. To her it felt like minutes, churning into hours, time slowed down, her death happening in slow motion.

"I'm gonna grab your head and push you down…"

She could no longer hear the words, her brain shutting down, her heart pumping blood loudly to her brain, desperately trying to keep her alive, to keep oxygen getting to where it was needed. She felt her body jerk and try to weakly pull away from the grip Jared had on her, but he kept her pushed down, the blue liquid flushing over her again and again as he pulled the chain a few more times.

The pounding in her head began to subside, a calmness floating through her body as stars danced in her minds eye. As the last lyrics were spoken, she fell peacefully into a forever sleep.

"I'm gonna flush the shit out of you!"

Chapter Four ... Whack a Mole Boy ...

Mario pounded on the door, frustrated and angry at himself for running after that witch. She was the devil incarnate, running through a door and magically locking it deadbolt behind her.

Maybe this was all a game to her? She knew where to run to because she was part of this sick, twisted shit?

And he felt the anger inside him rise even more at himself, instead of going back to Marielle to be with her he foolishly carried on, pushed through another door, and another, then another. His search for Leanne becoming his whole self, his new personality. The rage of what she had done thundering through his body. His body that was still feeling weak from the lightning shock that had torn away at his soul, but he needed to carry on, the get revenge on the girl that murdered his sister!

But now he was stuck! Stuck in a room that clearly was meant for him, this was his room of death and of course no Leanne in sight! A maze had led him here, a maze to disorientate, a maze created by some crazed witch.

The room was odd, a crudely set up pully system had been erected on the walls, chains and runners connected to a false ceiling, a ceiling that was full of man-sized holes. The ceiling housed nine holes, 3 x 3, and it was most definitely a recent addition to the building, it looked new, not as dusty or grimy compared to the rest of the building.

Mario had gingerly paced the room, knocking on the walls, trying the door, trying to find a way out. There looked to be an old light on the wall, it said something, written in an italic font but with it not lit up Mario couldn't make out what it read. There was also a random chair sat beneath one of the holes in the ceiling, it had been bolted to the floor, so it couldn't be moved.

As he walked the room he could hear a faint hum of music, a faint whisper of a female voice… Then nothing. His stomach dropped, a sense of dread filling his body. If there had been a song playing, then that possibly meant that someone else might be dead! He hoped that it was Leanne, that she had met her maker, but he also doubted it. Leanne was a sly witch and always managed to get out of sticky situations, it was like his Grandma always said to him, *"The devil looks after his own"*. And she had been right about most things, so he guessed it was true, Leanne had the devil's protection.

CLICK!

The sound echoed loudly in the room, and Mario looked up to where the noise had come from. One of the chains on the wall shivered.

SCREECH!

A metallic screech followed the click, and he watched in wonderment as the holey ceiling began to lower itself down on the runners and chains that had been attached to the walls. He walked back looking up, he tried to peer into one of the holes, but there was a gloomy darkness behind the ceiling that made it impossible to see.

"Whack a mole, Whack a boy, Whack a mole, Whack a boy, Whack a mole, Whack a boy..."

The song began in an instant, and with it an electrical surge and the light on the wall frizzed on, sparks flew from the twisted italic shapes, *'Whack a Mole'*.

It began to dawn on him what this room had become, a human sized 'Whack a mole' game! He had played one a few times at the fair back in the day... *but... what else did this have to do with him?*

"Whack a boy?" He questioned, looking around the now semi lit up space. Above one of the holes he could see it, a giant, wooden mallet like hammer that was huge, it had been engineered by someone with some skill, and it hung crudely to the ceiling above the false ceiling. Ropes and chains held it in place. His heart quickened in pace as he could tell that those ropes would pull the hammer back up to be released again and again, this was not a one-time hammer that he could try and dodge and be free. Oh no, he could feel it, this was going to be a long game.

Death's Carousel

"Always aiming the hammer at me, as your fist hit me down, down, down... You lift it again at me, so you can hit your final blow, blow, blow... You're a guy, but you think it's cool to pick on a girl, girl, girl, All for a girl that you make her hurl, hurl, hurl... If you dangle the hammer one more time, time, time, It'll end up where the sun doesn't shine, shine, shine..."

The girly voice echoed through the air, trying to hide the tinkering tell tale noises of the hammer being released. Mario heard it at the last second, the ceiling was low enough now that he had to duck and roll to be out of the hammer's way. SMACK! The hammer brushed past him, he felt the air vibrate from the force of the blow. It smacked into the floor cracking the tiles beneath it. Then as the song continued the hammer slowly began to be hoisted up back into place. A soft click let him know that it was locked in place and ready to strike again.

He gasped as he stood up, looking up to see the large weapon waiting, almost like it was holding its breath. *Surely it could only strike in one place? It was heavy, was the pully system that advanced that it could move along the holes? Or was it a game where they hoped he would make the mistake of just standing there in awe?* Well, he wasn't going to find out just standing there.

He moved slightly to one side, looking up through one of the holes, he kept his body low, just below the hole so he could move quickly. CLICK! The noise indicated the hammer's movement, and sure enough another rope tightened and sent the hammer hurtling to one side, the side where Mario stood waiting. At the last second in shock he sprung, rolling out of the way. The hammer smashed into the floor once again, splinters of floor tile and cement burst upwards and then fell littering the floor with jagged sharp chunks.

Sweat beaded on his brow and he wiped at it with his hand, "Shit", he said to no one in particular.

"I know my strength inside, is more than yours outside, I say whack a mole, whack a mole boy… You think you're stronger than me, but I have to disagree, whack a mole, whack a mole boy…"

Again, the hammer rose and again it fell. Crashing down hard just inches from where Mario had just been kneeling. The ropes being twisted and pulled to where he stood, like some giant puppet on giant strings. As it fell and smashed again and again like a record on repeat.

He laughed, this was just a workout for him like at the gym, he was hardly breaking too much of a sweat. The panic and sweat that he felt before was subsiding at how cumbersome the hammer was and how easy it was for him to roll out the way. Judging by the crudeness of the build, hopefully it would tear itself apart before too long and before it actually hit him.

"I'm not that little girl now, now, now, who's scared to go and tell now, now, now, I will show you power now, now, now, little whack a mole boy. You won the fight back then, how, how, how? With your fist pow, pow, pow, but I will fight back now, now, now, little whack a mole boy…"

All of a sudden, the song sped up, the tempo changing and the ceiling lunged down a few rungs more. "Ah shit", he exclaimed. It was now not so easy for him to duck and roll. The ceiling was forcing him into a lower crouch, lactic acid burned in his legs as he stayed crouching down, ready and waiting to move.

CLICK! BANG! The hammer came down hard and fast, Mario just manged to dive out the way. He fell down hard on one knee onto some rubble from the tiled floor. He cried out in pain. The sharpness of a sharp point stabbing at his kneecap and then the flow of warm blood gushing down his leg.

CLICK! CLICK! CLICK! The hammer lifted up again, and the holed ceiling clicked down another rung. It had become an almost evil limbo pole game.

"How low can you go?" he whispered to himself, trying to ease his now panic-stricken mind.

He peered out the hole, but could no longer see the hammer, the angle of the hole making it so he now had to stand up in a mid-crouch to see where it was. The false ceiling blocked out most of the light from the 'Whack a mole' light, the hammer hiding in the shadows like some demented bat.

This was going to be hard! He thought. With having to half stand he had to be extra quick when ducking down when the hammer fell and if he didn't duck or move fast enough… Well, it wasn't worth dwelling on, he just had to do it.

"Whack a mole, Whack a mole boy, Whack a mole, Whack a mole boy, Whack a mole, Whack a mole boy… Whack a boy… Wh, Wh, Whack a mole boy".

He stood, trying to anticipate the hammers next move, the pain in his leg searing. CLICK! It began to drop, right where Mario stood. He ducked but moved at an awkward angle, hitting his chin on the holed ceiling on the drop down, felt his teeth smash against each other, felt one snap under the pressure. He rolled just as the hammer hit down, a kind of shock wave of air pressure forcing him to fall onto his side.

He spat out his bloodied cracked tooth, felt his mouth with his tongue to find a few teeth had been chipped. But that had to wait, no point in worrying about it if he wasn't going to get out alive to see a dentist.

The hammer rose up, and he sat looking up, gasping for air and waiting.

"Hammers aren't always appropriate weapons, sometimes all that's needed is one perfect word, you punch and kick and spit at me, just to impress some girl, but you're not her boyfriend, and she doesn't want you, the perfect word is REVENGE!"

He listened to the words, revenge sounded so loud, and it cut deep. Someone was definitely out for revenge against him, and all of them. *But why a whack a mole?* He didn't hit girls, his Grandma and Mumma Bear bestowed that truthful knowledge on him from a young age. Said no matter what, you never hit a lady, no matter how much they upset you. And he lived by that mantra, he wanted to make them happy and proud of him… He never hit a girl… Never… *Only that one time, but she wasn't a girl she was a freak… She…Nancy… Nancy made me do it, I did it for Nancy!*

He sat there stunned, Kayella! This was all Kayella of course it was. Everyone who had picked on her was here. They had made her life hell and, she was the only girl he had ever laid a hand on. He hadn't been proud of it, no way… But he had done it none the less, and to appease a girl too. To please Nancy, to make her like him.

The flash back of her face hit him square in the gut, rendering him useless for a moment. Her tear and blood-stained face. Her eyes swelling up and black bruises appearing on her pale skin from his punches!

*   *   *

"Hey, Mario!" Marielle called from her room, "Yo, Idiot".

"What?" He called out back to his sister, and then skulking from his room putting his PS5 gaming controller down on his chair.

"Nancy's on the phone for you", she smirked.

"What?" he felt his cheeks burn from a blush as he grabbed the phone, "Yo Nancy, what's up?"

Marielle smirked even more and turned her head away shaking with a quiet laughter.

"Hey Mario, how's you?" Nancy's cool silky-smooth voice asked over the handset.

Mario felt that tingle of excitement that he got every time she so much as looked at him let alone spoke to him, but he tried to keep his voice as cool as hers, "I'm good, you?"

"Yeah, I'm ok I guess, but I need to ask a favour?" She asked ever so delicately.

Mario straightened up, the girl of his dreams was asking him for a favour, a million scenarios whizzed around his mind, *did she need bread picked up from the store, he wouldn't mind being invited in for a thank you, or her parcel got delivered to the wrong house, could he collect it and then come watch a film...* they all played out in his mind, these different scenarios of him and her... but what she did say shocked him and he wasn't quite expecting it. "Go on, what'da need?"

"The freak, I need her to get beaten up... I need you to beat her up for me!"

He stood there stunned for a moment, she wanted him to beat up a girl, to give another girl some whoop-ass. He sucked in his bottom lip and looked over at Marielle. Marielle shrugged as she couldn't hear the conversation and didn't know why he looked so perplexed. "You want me to beat up Kayella? The freaky girl?"

"Yes".

Marielle now sat up on her bed, she shook her head and mouthed the word 'NO' to her brother.

"What'da, she do to you?" He asked.

"She got me grounded and now I can't go to Leanne's party next month and my mum said I will probably be grounded when the prom comes around too!"

Mario's heart sunk, he had wanted to take Nancy to the prom. He hadn't officially asked her yet, but how could she refuse, she was asking him for favours and not just little ones, this was a big favour, so she must consider him at the very least a good friend and friends can go to the prom with one another.

"Was it cause of the Carousel thing?"

"Yeah... Because Leanne filmed me doing it and posted it online, which makes it look like it was only me picking on her and no one else, my parents want to bore the Devil out of me".

He sighed, "Why'd you even still hang with her after she incriminated you?"

"She's my friend", she said so matter of factly.

"But technically Leanne got you in trouble, not Kayella", he stated.

"Uh, take it you're not going to help me then", she pouted over the phone, sighing loudly so he could hear the annoyance.

"I didn't say that… But I'm just wondering why your beefing freaky girl and not Lee?"

"Me and Lee are fine, she apologised, but if Kayella had just… not existed then life would be fine".

Mario felt kinda bad for Kayella, the only reason their group hated on her was just due to her existing, being alive and, being poor and neglected. "I dunno how I feel about hitting a girl, Nancy. I mean, I'm a gentleman, I've been brought up with manners, you know".

"Ah don't worry about it, I'll ask Dan Vickers instead then, he'll do it, for me", she teased.

He glanced at his sister, again she sat there shaking her head, "No!" she whispered.

"Fine, I'll do it", he agreed. Dan 'Prince Charming' Vickers had all the girls fretting over him, and he too liked Nancy, a lot. Which obviously boiled Mario's blood. *There was no way she could do this, go running to him… What if she gave him the favours after the favours.* He shook himself mentally, that was not an image he wanted to see.

Marielle rolled her eyes and went back to her tablet, doom scrolling.

"Oh yay, thank you Mario, I knew you would do it for me", she said cheerily down the phone, "Ill phone Lee now and get her to plan how to do it, we need to lure her away from prying eyes".

"Ok", he said, the guilt filling his voice to the point it nearly broke.

"Well see you tomorrow at school. Then after school we will have our plan and do it. She won't get away with getting me in the shit". With that she put the phone down and Mario turned to face his sister's glare.

"You lovesick fool", she snapped, "Why do you let her use you?"

He shrugged.

"She is playin you! You think doing this will make her come running to you and fall head over heels in love? No... She playin...YOU!"

"I know, I know", He retorted, "But I have to try something to make her like me".

"Mario, bro, she won't ever like you that way, you don't have a vagina", She laughed.

He gave a sly yet shy grin, "I might be able to change her mind".

Once again Marielle shook her head, "That girl is in love with Leanne, that's why she let's her treat her like crap, and now you, well you're doing the same. It's like some weird fucked up love triangle".

Nancy held onto Mario's arm as they lay in wait in the deserted park. Leanne and Nancy had schemed all day of how to get her. Their best plan had been the walk home, Kayella usually walked through the park alone, an easy target, no one would see it or witness it, keeping Mario's reputation safe and also the rest of them.

Death's Carousel

Mario felt his heart hammer away in his chest, Nancy was so close to him, her soft hand gently placed on his bicep. The citrus scent of her perfume tickled his senses. Her warm breath on his neck as they sat hiding, keeping silent. Leanne was the other side of Nancy, and he noticed that Nancy had put her other hand on Leanne's leg, and she kept giving quick, longing glances in her direction. He knew his sister was right, but he had to hope, had to try to win her heart.

"What the fuck!" Leanne hissed.

Mario strained his neck to look out over the bush they hid behind, he could see Kayella, but she wasn't alone, she was walking with Tristan.

Nancy suddenly dropped her hands off both of them as Leanne stood up, her whole body shaking with rage.

Leanne stormed out of their hiding spot and 'rage' walked over to them as they slowly walked around the cobbled pathway that had pink and blue wispy flowers lining the edges. If rage hadn't been the emotion of choice, it could have looked quite romantic.

"What are you doing with her?" Leanne snapped at Tristan, she blocked both their way with her small angry frame.

Kayella immediately fell into a protective trance, her face dropped, her hair fell forward like a shield, her shoulders slumped, and it looked like all joy fell out of her soul.

"She's my friend Lee, what's wrong with that?" Tristan asked.

"Friend? Friend? Your friends with the freak!"

"Don't speak about her like that", he snapped back at her.

"I thought after last weekend that me and you had a thing!" Leanne said crossing her arms and pouting.

Tristan looked a little awkward, "I? What thing?"

"Me and you at the neighbourly barbeque? I thought we had a connection", she pouted.

"We do as friends", Tristan said.

"So, you call shoving your tongue down my throat a friend thing now?" She cried.

He held up his hands in defence, "What? We never…"

She stalked up to him and grabbed his shirt and pulled him away from Kayella, moaning furiously in his ear.

This left Kayella alone. She looked around the park and began to walk off, a complete look of confusion over her face. Nancy grabbed Mario's arm, "Now!"

They both jumped out of the bushes, Nancy running in front of Kayella to stop her from getting away, Mario behind her, crossing his arms trying to look threatening.

"I don't want any trouble", Kayella whined, her sweet melodic voice cracking with fear.

"Too late for that", Nancy hissed.

Kayella stared at Nancy, and Mario could see anguish there, not so long ago the two girls had been friends. Nancy, Marielle and Kayella, a threesome. But something happened, something had changed between them. Ever since Leanne had invited them round hers for a slumber party with her other bestie Sinead and a couple of other girls, it had all changed. They had begun meeting up, going to the shops together, sharing secrets and … Picking on Kayella. They had become almost carbon copies of Leanne, especially Nancy.

Which made him wonder why Marielle cared so much about his involvement, she had been just as mean to the 'Freaky' girl, if not more so than him. *Could it be she had grown a conscience and regretted her decisions… Nah…*

"Please", Kayella breathed, fear present in her shaking body and voice.

Nancy turned to Mario, "No one is here, do it now".

"Nancy I…I dunno", he began.

"What? You're betraying me", she hissed.

He shook his head, "No, no not at all… I just…"

"I'll go to prom with you", Nancy promised.

Mario's heart skipped a beat, "For real? I thought you were grounded for that too?"

She shrugged, "I was, but Leanne's mum spoke to mine and said it's a shame I can't make memories like my friends".

"But for sure, for truth yeah? Me and you will go together?"

She nodded, "Of course", and she laid one want hand on his arm, and looked deep into his eyes.

He nodded, "Ok". He turned to Kayella who stood like a little lost rabbit stuck in headlights, just waiting for what ever horror may come to her. He raised a hand and slapped her across the cheek.

A small, strangled cry of pain fell from her lips, full of shock and fear.

"Is that it?" Nancy looked pissed.

"Nah, nah, just getting started", he smiled.

For the next few minutes he pounded Kayella with his fists, he tried to hold back his full strength so as not to disfigure her too much or kill her, he'd heard of one punch kills, heard a kid a few years back had been done for a fight with a one punch kill. But he hit her enough to cause enough damage to appease Nancy. By the end of it Kayella's face was black and blue, her glasslike eyes wet with tears, blood stained her face from both his broken and cut knuckles and her nose and lip, both of which had split and were bleeding all over the place.

She crumpled to the floor weeping and sobbing. Mario knelt down to her, "It's nothing personal", he whispered.

*

The next day at school Kayella appeared in tutor time but the police and a social care team arrived, alerted by the school. They escorted her to a private room to talk, clearly it wasn't completely unknown that she was a child at risk with a grandparent with dementia and now other ailing illnesses and being a young carer.

Mario felt the guilt consume his body, his soul... *How could he have done this when her life was so hard as it was?*

Her face was puffy and deeply bruised, the cuts had butterfly stitches.

Mario sat shaking all day, sick to his stomach. He waited and waited for the police and the social services to come and question him, but no one came.

Eventually Kayella came back to class, she sat at the back and hid from everyone. The whispers began, people staring and gawping at her.

She never snitched…

Marielle took Mario by the arm as he left the school through the main door, "What the hell did you do to her bro?"

He looked sad, deep guilt spread over his face, "I didn't mean for it to be that bad".

"Why? Why'd you, do it?"

"She promised to go to prom with me", he replied.

Marielle rolled her eyes, "And you believe that playin bitch?"

Mario glanced over at Nancy who held on to Leanne's arm, they both walked straight past Mario, but neither acknowledged him. "I guess not", he replied.

"She used you again, she keeps using you. And for what, to hurt a girl…"

"Your one to talk", he laughed, "You flushed her head down the loo and burnt her".

Marielle looked away from him, "I know, and I regret it".

"Yeah, only cause you got your ass handed to you by mum".

"Not just that", she said quietly, "I just… We weren't brought up like that… To do these horrible things to someone else".

"And yet we still did em… We conformed to peer pressure", he sighed.

Just at that moment Kayella walked out of the school doors. She paused when she saw the two of them.

Panic rose in her face, in her eyes, the colour washed out of her already pale face. She steadied herself by grabbing the door handle. She shook her head, "No, not again".

Mario held up his hands, "I won't I promise, thanks for not snitching on me".

"Leave me alone", she cried and ran. She huddled her bag like a security blanket and charged out into the road, she weaved in and out of other students leaving, weaved in and out of moving cars, a few beeping at her as she blindly in a panic ran and with that, she was gone.

He looked at Marielle, "It was nothing personal".

"You try and tell her that", she said glumly, "We are all evil".

*   *   *

"I know my strength inside, is more than yours outside, I say whack a mole, whack a mole boy… You think your stronger than me, but I have to disagree, whack a mole, whack a mole boy…I'm not that little girl now, now, now, who's scared to go and tell now, now, now, little whack a mole boy, you won the fight back then, how, how, how? With your fist pow, pow, pow, but I will fight back now, now, now, little whack a mole boy".

The hammer came down fast, too fast, he ducked but not quick enough and the hammer came down hard and fast onto his shoulder. It knocked him flying to the floor, jagged pieces of tile clawing at his abdomen as he then tried to claw himself back up onto his feet.

Winded he stood, bracing himself as the hammer rose once again.

Death's Carousel

His shoulder felt bruised, fractured, maybe even broken in places, but he could still move it, just.

"Whack a mole, whack a mole boy, what a mole, whack a mole boy, whack a mole, whack a mole boy, oh whack a mole boy".

His lungs gasped for air, his shoulder screamed in pain, and he was tired. Something inside him began to give up, he knew Marielle was gone, he knew when he ran after Leanne, that she was dead no matter what. He was such a stupid fool, all those years ago and again now, his foolish actions were getting people hurt, either by his hand directly or indirectly.

All those years of chasing Nancy, even to this day he still pined after her. Nancy had been the girl of his dreams, once upon a time she had been kind and sweet, but then she met Leanne and everything about her changed. But then, Leanne had changed them all. Over the years their group had remained close, maybe by the trauma they shared of what despicable things they had done, no one new entered their group, why would they, they had been known as the bullies, and in a small-town people talk and know everyone's business.

They pretended to be happy, a big family made by friends, but deep below the surface they were just all bully's that couldn't befriend anyone else as everyone knew their pasts. They couldn't get out even if they wanted to.

Mario had made up his mind, he was going to join his sister. He walked over to the chair that sat bolted to the floor and sat down, his head in his hands as he wept.

"I'm not that little girl now, now, now, who's scared to go and tell now, now, now, I will show you power now, now, now, little whack a mole boy, you won the fight back then how, how, how? With your fists pow, pow, pow, but I will fight back now… Little whack a mole boy".

The last verse sung, just the bridge left to go, the music seemed to slow down with time as the hammer slowly rose for its final blow. He felt so defeated as the huge weapon clicked into place, the guilt had eaten away at him for years but now, it had finally come to blow. He hated himself so much for what he had done.

CLICK! The hammer fully in position.

"Ahh, Ahh, Whack a mole boy…"

CLICK! BURRRRR the mechanical device turned to aim the hammer at the desired killing position.

"Ahh, Ah, Whack a mole boy…"

CLICK! SWOOOSH! The hammer fell in release.

"Ahh, Ahh, Whack a mole boy…"

SWOOSH! Air being forced sideways.

"Come on you fucker! Take me…"

"Ahh. Ahh, Whack a mole, Whack a mole…"

SPLAT!!! "ARGHHHH!"

"Boy…"

The hammer crunched down on Mario's skull and crushed it in hard. What was left of his teeth shattered upon impact, disintegrating into bony dust. His skull exploded into shards of bony matter, splatters of grey and pink brain tissue and flesh slopped up the wall behind him, some landing on the hot whack a mole light, sizzles of hot meat cooking, creating a smoking stench of death.

Death's Carousel

The force of the skull exploding caused an eyeball to pop out from its socket. His whole body sagged in the chair as other bodily fluids leaked out, plastering him in place.

Then the door squeaked open…

"It's Nothing Personal".

Chapter Five ... Bumper car Tag, Dodgem hide and seek...

Luke Godden awoke with a start, his mouth dry, his body aching. His sleep had not been a peaceful one, he had been laying awkwardly, squished up, his legs and arms tucked in, his back arched. It was all dark around him, he was in a room that was not quite a room. It was small, tiny, more like a box. It smelt like oil and diesel, like a mechanics workshop.

He tried to remember where he was, tried to recall what had happened... Flashes came back to him, quick colourful flashes...

Wine, lots of wine. The guys had all been together, partying, music had been playing in the background, the smell of food wafted in the air. Wine, more wine... Then everyone had started to crash out, to collapse, to fall asleep... on the floor.

A woman, and a man. Both hooded in cloaks, grabbing them all, tying their hands, binding their legs so they couldn't move, but no one moved, the drugs were too strong.

Wine... Poison, drugs in the wine!

A screech of tyres, his eyes fluttering as he came to for a brief split second, seeing the back of a van, turning a corner, he slid around hitting his head, then darkness came for him again.

Then the motion of being lifted, pulled around, dragged across hard floor, things snagging his clothes, tugging at his skin, grazing his elbows.

Hard cold cuffs being clamped to his wrists, being hurled into... into a room, no a box... no... A boot of a car!

Such a weird dream, yet it wasn't a dream at all. He was awake and he was in a car boot, cramped up and cuffed.

He panicked thrashing around, kicking the boot, trying to punch the boot but his cuffed hands prevented him from doing any damage, then he tried to stay calm, trying to breathe but he was hyperventilating, he couldn't get his breath in, there was no air... no air! Darkness...

Some time passed and Luke came to again, but he felt different, something had changed... He opened his eyes and winced as bright dancing lights flickered all around him. A collage of pinks, greens, yellows and blues, blending into purples, reds and oranges... There was also static noise, like a record player left with the needle on once it had finished.

He tried to move but the cuffs were still on him and now tied to something else. He wearily looked around him, "What the?" He sat in a bumper car, a fairground dodgem.

His hands had been cuffed to the steering wheel. Confused he called out, "Hello? Guys? Anyone there?"

But only silence greeted him.

"Lee? Mario? Haha very funny…" But still no one replied.

Sniffing uncomfortably as a cold chill had encased him, he looked around the dodgem ride, hoping to see the ride operator, but the place looked wrong, abandoned. The ride itself had decayed, like it had been left for a good few years, plants had pierced their way through and began to grow upwards, spiralling up the pillars that housed the roof of the ride. He noticed also that his was the only actually dodgem on the platform of the ride, his metal tail that forked up to the metal sheet that conducted the electricity was the only one connected.

THUD-DUNK!

He spun his head to the noise, a lone can of fizzy pop rolled across the floor, as if someone had kicked it.

"Er… Hello?"

Nothing.

"This ain't funny, I want off now", he moaned.

The static of the record scraped as if a needle was indeed being pulled across it, then a tune began to play. The dodgem car itself had a speaker set into the steering control panel, as well as some extra speakers hanging from the roof. The tune got louder and louder, in different circumstances, Luke would have raved to this banger of a tune, but at that moment in time he felt weird, uneasy, a sense of dread.

A small puff of stage smoke hissed in the air to one end of the platform, and a lone female figure appeared. She wore a long dark cloak, her hood up and covering her face. She held a microphone and let one of her delicate fingers slide down and press a button. An alarm sounded out, one that signalled the start of the ride.

The car he sat in spurred to life and jolted forward, he grabbed the steering wheel in front of him, dread but a sick sort of amusement fluttered through him, like a hundred butterfly kisses, but he quickly realised he had no control over the small vehicle whatsoever. He zoomed around the amusement arena, lights flashing fast, distorting his vision as he tried to peer out past the ride and into the rest of the amusement park.

"Riding in your daddy's Audi... You pulled up to me, said howdy, I like you, think your real dead cute, can't tell my friends or they'll execute... me... Speeding in the multistorey, things about to get really gory, you have no license to thrill, but I have a license to kill... you..."

That voice, he knew it, that sweet, melodic voice that had called to him in so many of his dreams and fantasies, "Kayella", he cooed as the girl came into view.

She pulled down her hood and blew him a kiss, she was stunning, even better than he remembered her, she had grown and glown up. Her eyes held a mischievous sparkle that he had never seen in them before, it was a sparkle he wanted to reach out and touch.

As his car zoomed past her, she began to dance, almost erotic, *had she finally given in? Had she finally decided to take a chance on him like he had always wanted?* His eyes fixated on her, like they had so, so many times before. She lifted her arms, swung her hips, and he licked his lips, like a hungry predator waiting for his prey.

He had adored her, he would have bathed her feet in milk and honey and with his own hair cleaned them and even kissed them if she had let him.

As she sung, her sweet, melodic voice sticking in his teeth, he remembered in the music rooms at school, how he would stand at the small round window and watch her, watch as her mouth produced sweet, sweet music. Music, he wanted to capture and make his own.

She should have been a star, with a voice like hers she should have been so confident, happy and snatched up by a record label, or by him. *No, not a star, she should have been all his… A star only for him, for no one else… She should have burned bright for his eyes only…* But the bullying from the others, from Leanne… He looked down at his cuffed hands, if Leanne hadn't had such power, then that sweet girl would have been his already. But she made everyone's life hell, that if they so much as smiled at Kayella, hell would rise up from the Earth's crust and devour them all… He couldn't imagine what she would have done to him if she found out he was in love with her… In love with the freaky girl!

She twisted and twirled, her long glossy hair flipping round her, it was luscious and ran down her back like a dark waterfall. He leered at her as he zoomed past her again, he tried to reach out to her, he wanted to feel her soft skin beneath his fingers, to wrap her hair around his fingers. He felt so giddy with the prospect that his obsession as a teenager might finally become a reality.

He sighed inwardly, *why had he given a crap what the others had thought so much? Leanne, Nancy, Mario and the rest, why had he cared.* He had put Kayella on a pedestal, he worshipped the ground she walked on, but he could never reveal that part of him to them. Instead, he had to pretend to stalk her, to harass her, to make her life uncomfortable so the others would accept him.

When all he had wanted was for her to be his, for her to be his life, his every breath.

Swooshing past her he could almost smell her, the sweet, tasty aroma of her skin, sweet like berry flavoured icing, sweet like nothing he had ever experienced before. As he zoomed past his car twirled and turned him to face away from her momentarily, but it was enough to see a rather unkempt group of people standing to one side. No not people, freaks! Robotic, Animatronic freaks!

Their outfits where of mascots, a yellow duck, a grey wolf and a brown moose, but they were decayed, dishevelled... Animatronics, robots, he could see the veins of their robotic parts, the oiled blood pustulating from torn seams and shredded fabric. They had been mascots of the local school, college and university sports teams.

Once upon a time the fairground had been a bustling place for teen, uni and college students to hang out. Many a great night had been cheering on their local sports team, the dancing electronic mascots as one team, showing how the town was united no matter what, even when they played against one another. But now, now the mascots looked creepy, decayed, even monstrous, not something you would want to bump into in a dark alley on a dark and gloomy night.

The tempo of the song shifted, the lights above the animatronics burst to life and in turn the rusted, broken robots woke up from their slumber. Their arms and legs gyrating to the beat of the music, their dull lifeless eyes wobbling around in their rusted skulls, staring at him, looking into his soul.

"Bumping cars in the car park, it's late, it's getting pretty dark, bumper car tag, dodgem hide and seek, not getting kidnapped is looking pretty bleak… Pushed the throttle, pulled the choke, you dragged me off in a cloud of smoke… Bumper car tag, dodgem hide and seek, you lock me in the boot so I cannot speak… Tyres screaming, tyres screeching, vibrating in the sky… Electricity powering as the dodgems fly… Bumper car tag, dodgem hide and seek…"

She sang the words with such conviction, he knew she sung them only for him. He almost drooled over her every syllable.

He remembered the night she sang about as if it was just yesterday…

*   *   *

He waited, waited in the darkness of the shadows on the second story of the multistorey car park in the centre of town. The lights were on sensors and only flicked on when a car or person walked under one. But if someone was to park and not move, then the lights would turn off, engulfing the car park in darkness. People had argued when they changed from on all the time to sensors, especially women that it made things dangerous, that those that shopped late or left work in the dark were at risk. *At risk of what?* He scoffed to himself. People liked surprises, especially girls. Someone waiting for you in the dead of night, the pitchest

Death's Carousel

of blacks was just a nice surprise, it showed they cared, that they really thought about you and what they wanted to do to you.

    Checking his watch, he saw the time read 5.45pm and at this time of year meant it was already dark out. It also which meant in a few minutes she would leave her small-time job. He didn't understand why she worked there, she should be one of those kept at home, a kept woman, a housewife, like his own mother. He would make her one soon, one day he would be the man of the house and have a job to take care of her. But for now, his dad gave him money, made sure he was taken care of… But one day she would be his and she would sing just for him.

    The door to the car park opened and in she walked, she looked tired, bending down to rub her aching feet. She worked in the local music and record shop, selling musical instruments, records, CD's and giving singing lessons to the local children. She had originally gone for a job in the local haberdashery, where linens, fabrics, curtains, duvets, and handmade clothes were made and sold, but due to her hand injury she hadn't been accepted as she struggled with scissors and sewing tasks, instead she settled for her next passion, music. He knew all of this, he knew everything about her, probably more than she even knew about herself.

    She walked down, passing his car in the shadows, she didn't notice him watching and waiting. She made it to her car, an old banger, one door was peeling and rusted, it had dents all down it and all the tyres were of different makes. He felt a bitter taste brew in his mouth, he was a little wary of a girl that could drive, that were modern, free thinkers and independent, and made out they didn't need a man, but he could change that, he would make it so she needed him, and him alone.

Fumbling in her bag for her keys he watched, waited and then leant on the horn.

HONK!

The loud noise echoed violently in the car park, bouncing off the walls, causing her to jump out of her skin, her keys flying out her hands and clattering onto the cement floor. She flung her head round scanning the darkness.

FLASH! He turned on his headlights full beam, the instant flood of lights caused her to fall back, her hand going over her eyes to try and protect them.

VROOM! VROOM! He revved the engine in true boy racer fashion. Fear and panic flashed over her face, her eyes, her dark piercing eyes… They called to him to help her.

He slammed his foot to the pedal and the car lurched forward, screeching as he turned the wheel sharply and pulling up the handbrake to turn the car.

She ran!

Flight instead of fight took over her, and she bolted heading back the way she had come, heading to the door to lead back down into the mall. He couldn't have that, couldn't have her escape, the chase was on. She clearly wanted this, to be chased, to be caught, to be dominated. The excitement spurred him on, he almost didn't hear himself laugh with glee over the sound of screaming tyres.

She was nearly to the exit, so he sped up, she glanced behind her and froze, seeing that he wasn't going to stop. She turned another direction and stumbled over her own feet, falling hard on her knees and hands.

Death's Carousel

He was so busy watching her run the other way he didn't see the parked car before it was too late... BANG!

"Oh shit", he said in an angry panic. He stopped the car and got out to inspect the damage, "No, no, no!" He flung his hands to his head in frustration.

The Audi had a large dent in the front bumper and along the side wing, "No, no, my dad is gonna kill me", he hissed through gritted teeth. He felt panic, fear and anger cascade down his body. Then he looked at Kayella, "You... You... If you hadn't of run none of this would have happened! You made me chase you".

Kayella stayed tucked away by another parked car, he could see her, but if he tried to run and grab her, she could dart either side of the parked vehicle, he couldn't let her potentially get away, he had to time this right.

"You want to be chased, I'll chase you", he smiled, a sudden madness riveting through his eyes.

"No", she tried to say confidently but it came out as a mere squeak, "No... I don't want to be chased, I didn't want to be chased, you came here to me, I didn't ask for this".

He seethed inside, now she was gas lighting him, making him think it was his fault when she clearly had run to make him chase her. He moved, a quick fluid motion in her direction. She dodged to one side, flitting away to the left, but he anticipated her decision and lunged left, his fingers just reaching her arm, grasping it tightly and pulling her towards him.

"Nooo!" She screamed.

She kicked and wailed as he drew her in close to him, "Look calm down", he breathed, "It's ok I'm here now. It's ok I know you didn't mean to do this, it was an accident, I know my dad will understand, you can just pay him off monthly, a percentage of your wages".

"What?" She said confused, "You crashed the car not me".

Anger spread over his face and his grasp on her wrist tightened, "You made me do it, you ran…"

"I ran because you scared me, not because I wanted to be chased".

He shook his head, "You lie, don't lie to me…"

She trembled in his hand, he could almost taste her fear, a sweet little hit on his tongue, intoxicating like a drug. Without thinking he leaned in to kiss her, his mouth encased hers, his hand pulling her in close.

Pain, sharp pain ripped through his mouth, then the taste of iron. She'd bit him and bit him hard drawing blood.

He pushed her away, putting his hand to his mouth, "You bit me!" he sounded so hurt, so pained, almost on the verge of tears.

"I didn't consent to you kissing and touching me", She said matter of factly.

"This is all wrong", he moaned, "You were meant to fall in love with me, to let me protect you, own you…"

"I don't need to be owned", she whispered.

"Really?" He hissed, he was so madly in love with her, *how could she not see it, want it or understand it?* "Well, your mine now", He gripped her arm once again and dragged her to the car.

"Get off me!" She screamed.

He stayed silent as he pushed a button to unlock the boot of the car, he grabbed her hair and pulled her down, pushing her into the car. She screamed louder, kicking and scratching, screaming and biting at him.

BANG! He slammed the boot shut, sweat burrowing over his top lip, congealing with his warm blood that pumped out through the teeth marks.

"Let her go!" A female voice commanded behind him.

He turned to see a middle-aged man and woman standing a few feet away, they had clearly heard the commotion and come running to have a nose, Shit!

"Let who go?" he feigned ignorance.

"Don't play the fool", the man snapped, his smooth cut silver fox hair gave him an authoritative look.

"She's the fool!" He snarled, "All I wanted was to look after her and care for her".

The woman tried a gentler approach, "Is everything ok son? You seem... Out of sorts?"

"I'm not your son!" he exclaimed, *what did she think he was crazy?*

"I didn't mean son, like my boy, it's a figure of speech, like son, sonny Jim", she looked at the man beside her, "I think he needs help, he seems a little, delusional".

"Delusional?" He gasped, "No ma'am I am not! I am the respected son of Patrick Godden, he's the..."

"Manager at the factory in town", the man finished.

Luke nodded, "You know him?"

The man nodded back, "Yes I do".

"Well then you know the power he has", Luke smirked.

The man looked at the woman, her long brown hair had hidden silver strands weaved into it and it blew in the cool breeze that had swept into the car park, "Everyone knows his son isn't the full ticket… I think we should call Pat and…"

"No, no there is no calling my dad!"

"Look son you are clearly having some form of mental break down, kidnapping a girl is not right, it's not on".

"Liar! She's my girlfriend".

"Well, if that is true then that is no way to treat your girlfriend, is it?"

"Well, we are going for a drive", he retorted.

"With her in the boot of the car? That can't be very comfortable for her?" The woman cooed gently.

"She likes it, says it's fun", he lied.

"Look, let's just call your dad, I don't think you're in a fit state to drive".

"State? What? I haven't been drinking, I haven't taken anything… I can drive… He let's me use his car all the time".

"I don't think he does now does he? I think you just take it", the man said.

Luke felt annoyed, confused, of course his dad let him take the car, he used it all the time. "Screw you guys", he snapped and hopped into the car. The man lunged forward trying to unlock the boot, but Luke knew what he would do, so he hit the button to lock all the doors. He revved the engine and put it in gear and sped off, ramming the handbrake up to spin the car in a cloud of screeching, tyre fraying smoke.

Excitement fuelled his body, adrenaline making his legs and arms do all the work without him needing to think.

Death's Carousel

He raced around the car park, speeding round the parked cars, flying down the ramps towards the exit.

Headlights shone in the rear-view mirror. That damned interfering couple, they were coming for him, they wanted to take Kayella away from him, wanted her for themselves. Well, he wasn't about to let that happen!

He sped out of the car park, smashing the car into the barrier, splinters of plastic rained down over the car and the road. Not caring about the car anymore, he raced off in a cloud of petrol induced smoke, the car was damaged anyway, and Kayella would just have to pay to have it fixed. Yes, his dad would be mad, but he would understand, he always understood.

Sparks flew from the chassis as it scraped over a speed bump, a corner came up fast, a red light on the traffic-controlled road. He didn't look, he just put his foot down and raced through the intersection. BEEP! An angry driver coming from the right where it was a green light, screeching as they hit the brakes, but Luke didn't care, the thrill was exciting.

The headlights from the couple's car were blinding as they raced behind him, they kept beeping at him, the woman even wound down the window and pleaded with him to stop, to think about the girl, they just wanted to talk. But he knew their plan, they wanted to take her away from him, that thought made him angrier, and his foot hit the pedal harder.

A park was up ahead, it had a dirt path that ran through it, not really meant for cars but he needed to lose the losers on his tail. Not caring about what might be ahead he mounted the pavement and zoomed into the park via the large open gate, sparks flew again as the metal from the gates scraped the side panels of the car. The windows shook with the pressure as he squeezed the car through, one cracking, zig zag lines spidering up the glass.

He could just make out the dirt path through the throng of trees and greenery, he could have sworn the path had once been bigger and wider than this when he'd walked it as a child with his dad. But he didn't care, all he needed was to get to the other side and he would be free. The park led out to the other side of town, but the car of the losers would have to go the long way round, a five-minute round trip, whereas he could see the exit just ahead, he was nearly there and… A DOG! A BLOODY DOG APPEARED!

A dog ran out in front of the car, a Great Dane, on a running lead, *where the hell was the owner? Why was it so far out in the park? Why didn't they keep the stupid thing on a shorter lead?* Luke swerved, the steering wheel pulling sharply to the left. He fought with it, just missing the dog by mere inches. A furious scream, the owner was suddenly in the head lights, they jumped, dove out of the way. Again, he turned the steering wheel sharply. The car jolted and was suddenly on two wheels, he'd hit a raised flower bed that had propelled the car up, two wheels in the air, the other two straddling the ground, cutting chunks out of the soil. BANG! The car stomped back down onto the ground, a little scream sounded out from the boot, he looked in the mirror, of course he couldn't see her, but it was a natural instinct to look, to take his eyes off the path… CRUNCH… BANG!!!

Tick, Tick, Tick… The car was silent other than the faint ticking of hot metal that had come to a sudden stop.

Death's Carousel

Luke's head hurt, warmth was flowing down his face. He looked in the mirror to see blood pumping from a cut on his forehead, he'd hit the windscreen and left a nice crack, the glass had shattered from the impact.

KAYELLA! He felt sick to his stomach, *was she hurt? Had he hurt her? Would she be, ok? Would she forgive his foolish actions?*

He tried the door, but it was crumpled from the impact and refused to open. Leaning over to the passenger side he pulled the handle. With a creak and cry it opened, he scrambled from the car, falling to his knees and cracking them on the gravel and soil that the car had spun and dug up. The fresh night air filled his lungs, the smell of the soil, mixed with petrol and hot acrid metal.

"There! Oh my gosh he crashed the car!" A female voice called out, the same voice of the woman from the car park.

"It's ok the police are on their way", a new female voice added, *maybe the dog walker?* "Bloody maniac nearly killed me and my dog".

"He has a girl in the boot, he kidnapped a girl!" A male's voice sounded out.

"What!" the second female, "Yes you heard that right". She was clearly still on the phone to the police, "Yes, they said he kidnapped a girl… We're going to need an ambulance too, the car is totalled".

Luke sat there frozen, he didn't want to leave Kayella, she was his, he had taken her to protect her, to make her his. But once the police came, they would take her away anyway. Before he knew what he was doing he was running, running out of the park, running down the road... Running, running... running...

*

A few days had passed since the crash and Luke sat in a police cell, his lawyer talking him through the process of what would happen next.

He would be going to court, on counts of kidnap and causing injury and being a danger to life by careless driving and with no insurance as it was his dad's car and not insured for him. With multiple witnesses there was no chance for a plea for innocence. Instead, he would be pleading guilty pending a mental health assessment. They might be able to reduced his sentence on the grounds of mental health as he's clearly had some form of brain malfunction. But that would also mean once his sentence was done that a restraining order would be against him, he would not be able to contact Kayella again. That was what hurt him the most...

*   *   *

That had been four years ago, he had served his sentence, three and half years. He'd been out six months now, would have been sooner but the psychologist wouldn't sign him off, stating his 'still' very much rampant obsession with the girl posed a risk to his and her health. His dad had spoken to him, persuaded him to not mention Kayella to his therapist anymore. And sure enough, he stopped speaking about her and acted normal and voila, he was released.

And they had to admit, he'd been good, not once had he gone to her... Well, not that she would know! He knew she was doing good, her singing career was taking off, he knew she had a record label wanting to work with her and that very soon she would be leaving their gloomy little town. His heart had broken, knowing she was leaving was hurtful, but now she was here, she had him, of course she wouldn't leave him, how could she, they were meant to be!

"Cotton Candy hangs in the air, we would make a real great pair, secrecy to hide our relationship, if they find out, I'll have no friendship…"

She sung the verse with such soul and courage, he knew that no one would be accepting of their relationship, but that didn't matter, as long as they had one another they needed no one else.

As her mouth moved with every syllable, he remembered what it was like to have his mouth on hers. He brought his fingers up to trace the tiny tooth like scars that lined his bottom lip where she had bit him all those years ago. He had picked at the scabs to make sure they stayed, as a true memory and reminder of her. A little bit of her with him always.

She danced and moved, her slender legs prancing to where the animatronics danced, she sang as she danced and swayed around the decomposing robotics. "Bumping cars in the park, it's late, it's getting pretty dark, other than the metal spark, Bumper car tag, Dodgem hide and seek… Pushed the throttle, pulled the choke, you dragged me off in a cloud of smoke, Bumper car tag, Dodgem hide and seek, Tyres screaming, Tyres screeching, vibrating in the sky... Electricity powering as the dodgems fly... I will smile as I watch you fry... Bumper car tag, Dodgem hide and seek..."

His brow furrowed in confusion, *watch as I fry? What did she mean? Did she think he was hot or...*

His blood ran cold as one of the animatronics had been holding something, something dangerous. It was a dark green almost black weapon, something he had seen on the video games he had played and enjoyed, it was a weapon that was deadly and would indeed make him fry.

"A rocket launcher... Kayella, sweetheart, darling... That's not a toy you should be playing with!" His voice cracked with a newfound fear, she wasn't accepting him into her life at all, she was about to blast him out of it forever.

She smiled, a grin that was so utterly wicked, something he had never seen cross the face of his darling Kayella before. Her sweetness was dissolving before his very eyes, a darkness was sweeping through her, taking her over...

How on earth had she got herself hold of one of them? She was sweet, innocent... How could she access weapons like that? That was like illegal black-market shit!

She lifted the rocket launcher and swung her hips, she was using it like a dance partner. She swung one arm up, flipped her hair, made her hips move in ways Luke had only ever dreamt of. Her once delicate arms looked strong, and they moved with a grace of someone who knew what they were doing. Cradling the weapon, one arm wrapped around it like it had a waist, then she spun it and cradled it again.

"Bumper car tag... Dodgem hide and seek..."

She spun, her heeled shoes clacking on the floor, she spun again, the weapon spinning on the spot, a very good dance partner, it took her dominance with no fight. She spun the other way, lifting the weapon with more purpose, lifting it up to her shoulder, holding it like one of his video game characters.

"Bumper car tag... Dodgem hide and seek... And now I seek you out, my fire and rage pour out the spout..."

She took aim at him, his car coming to a startling halt. He couldn't move, his panic froze him to the spot, he didn't even think to try to shake or move the cuffs, to try and escape.

"Fire burning, scalding me... As I'm trying to break free... If she flees just let her be, fire burning..."

He'd heard from his Lawyer that Kayella had indeed incurred a burn wound, the car had become hot and overheated after the crash, and that as he ran away in panic, the couple and the dog walker had fought bravely to rescue her, even as the car sparked into flames, threatening to trail to the fuel tank, threatening to blow his beloved to smithereens, and now, she was repaying that threat.

SWOOSH! The air felt warm before the fiery rocket smashed into him, the air rippled with heat, making lines in the air before a fiery wall enveloped him, a blanket full of heat and pain. "Scalding me..." She carried on singing as he screamed out in pain, his flesh burning, charring and melting from his body, "As your trying to break free, as you flee, I won't let you be... I'll repeat what you did to me... Bumper car tag... Dodgem hide and seek!"

Her laughed crackled through the air as the smell of cooked meat wafted around her, not once did she falter, unlike him. Tears dried instantly as they fell from his eyes, disappearing in a mixture of stream and rage. As his body collapsed in on itself, he saw the final moments of her song, of her fiery performance and died in wonderment at the girl who used to be so weak but was now stronger than them all.

She took aim again, placing another rocket into the weapon, she sent it flying into the animatronics. Fire burst up all around them, but still they danced, their wiring melting as one, frying inside. Their gears grinded to a stabbing halt as the fire stripped away any grease and oils that kept them agile, and moving. Their fabric, their fake fur shrivelling up in a cloud of toxic smoke. As her song came to a close, her final verse being sung, their movements slowed, their dance creaking and scraping to an end.

"Bumping cars in the car park, It's late, it's getting pretty dark, bumper car tag... Dodgem hide and seek..."

*

Kayella watched in amazement as the flames engulfed the once unstable stalker that had terrorized her for months and months of her teenage years. He had showed her how dangerous obsession could be. The crash had been one of the scariest things to have happened in her life. To be encased in a dark box, to hear the world whipping past, to then hear and feel metal crunching, breaking and compacting under a horse powered force. The car heating up, no air, making her feel like she was burning alive.

The smell of cooked human meat was like nothing else she had experienced before, but it was a scent she would remember for the rest of her life, it was the smell of victory, the scent of success. She felt so strong, so unstoppable…Her whole life had been a disappointment, people screwing her over, bullying her, tormenting her, terrorising her, rejecting her, her own parents not wanting her, not being born a boy to carry on the family name, jobs turning her away because she was shy, because of the people that knew her and spewed lies, no one believing in her, no one loving her… But everything was changing, after today her life would be better. Some of those that had wronged her would be gone, dead… no longer able to have power over her, she would be free. She would be powerful, she would be the one in control of her life from this day forward.

She spun on her heel, carrying the rocket launcher over her shoulder, the weight of it made her feel strong, stronger than anyone could have anticipated her to be.

Tristan walked out of the gloom, and she handed the heavy weapon to him. He looked deep into her eyes for a brief moment. He knew their plan, knew what had to be done… But he didn't know about her plan for her own happy ever after, and he wouldn't, not until she wanted him to.

Chapter Six ... Punch and Judy...

Kayella marched into the room that had become their base. Computer screens were lined up on one wall from the previous security team that had been paid to watch over the dead theme park, but now the ones that still had life in them were rigged up to the system Tristan had set up.

She tapped a few buttons and watched as Tristan set out to work preparing their 'Final' performance. She couldn't wait, she was excited, Leanne and Jared would finally get their comeuppance. Leanne had ruined her childhood, her teenage years and with Jared's help was even trying to ruin any chances she had in her adult life. But she would live or well die... to regret it all. Leanne's days were numbered, and it made Kayella feel so alive inside. For years she had been a ghost of herself, being shy, keeping everything inside, feeling like the only way out was to become nothing, to become no one, to be forgotten… But not anymore!

Her singing career was about to take off, a record label had signed her, she was about to move across the country away from the hell hole that was her hometown of Rivervalle. Someone had heard her voice, heard the voice of the true calculating Kayella, not the shy, rigid and bullied one. They had said her voice was sweetly unique, and that her vibe was dark, moody and sultry, that they needed someone like her on the music market. She had a niche that no one else had at that time and they could see the potential.

At first, she had been scared, afraid… Sending off her mix tape to be judged… She was always judged, always looked down upon and rejected. But they had seen the true her… But there was one thing holding her back… Her lifelong tormentors! They would surely try to ruin it all for her, they would contact magazines, pretending to be friends of hers, then they would lie… Expose her for the bullied version of her that her hometown knew her for. Then people would laugh, *why would they buy or listen to music of a freak?* They wouldn't… She would flop, her music branded freaky and dire embarrassing. She couldn't handle that… they had already taken her love of fashion and needlework away from her. Her hands damaged, the muscle cut so deep her hands no longer able to cope with the motion of sewing. *They would not steal this from her!* They were loose ends, and they needed unpicking, cutting up and throwing away. Their lives meaningless, their evil ways to end… They would ruin her life no more, they would ruin no one else's life… She was the saviour, the kindred spirit to exhume their souls and deliver them unto the hellish demons they belonged to.

She believed in no god, no god would let someone be bullied to the point of life seeming worthless and pointless, no god would make it, so she had no one, no friends, no family, not her cousin, not even her own nanna, her mind taken by illness... That's just evil... If there was a god, he was a damned evil one.

But there was a higher power, a higher plane that she had tapped into mentally, it had awoken in her, she knew she could do this. Take a stand and succeed.

Tristan was nearly complete with the stage set up. Butterflies flitted around her stomach, this needed to be her best performance yet... It was all practice for when she took to the big stage.

She left the monitor room and made her way to where Tristan resided. It had seemed their paths crossing all those years ago and then again, just those few months ago were meant to have been. He was meant to find her and help her. But deep inside she still lacked trust towards him...

She breathed in fresh air that was tinged with the hint of death and fire. It might not be long until someone noticed a fire at the old Riverside Fun Fair, so she had to make sure that things ran on a timely manner. The stage was set to perfection. Two unmoving figures lay on the floor outside of the House of Mirrors. The mirrored roof that hung over the entrance made a great structure to house the rigs and pullies for the special effects for the next song. The two figures had ropes tied to each of them, with bows and ribbons to 'beautify' it, or just to let them know how crazy she was feeling and had become, it was a stupid accessory to add, but she was trialling things for her true, real performances for when she would eventually go on tour.

Both figures lay sleeping peacefully, but not for long. Their bodies entwined within one another, holding each other, so close, too close, almost like they were glued at the hip!

She turned to Tristan, his wide eyes staring at her, a filter of fear weaving into them as he looked upon the new Kayella. "You ready?" She asked him, softly but with a hint of commanding authority in her voice.

He nodded, "Always".

She smiled but it didn't reach her eyes. She wished Tristan had 'always' been ready, but truth be told he hadn't been ready, and deep inside he still wasn't.

She remembered the tender looks and touches of hands holding hands. She remembered him coming to her aid on a few occasions when Leanne and her cronies had wronged her. But ultimately, he had been brainwashed by Leanne. Sucked in to believe her lies, sucked in to a kind of 'Stockholm Syndrome' where he had fallen in love with the enemy, the manipulator, the person who held his heart hostage.

She shook away the memories, it didn't serve her well now to be sentimental, to relive the past with him. What she needed to focus on now was the future, her future and to leave no loose ends.

*

Leanne woke up, dazed and groggy and again feeling like she was tied to something. She was getting fed up with these games now and it was making her angry.

She opened her blurry eyes, she could see two figures standing to one side out of the corner of her eye. Kayella and Tristan! Her mouth went dry as she eyed them both.

Of course! How did she not see it sooner! The Carousel and Nancy... Sinead and the Bouncy Castle... Mario beaten by the hammer... Marielle in a bathroom... Now for her and Jared! She felt sick to her stomach, there were many ways in which Kayella could murder her, and it relate to something Leanne had done to her... *Which would she choose? And Jared? She knew about him refusing her a house sale but death by house? And if she was desperate to buy why not just buy a house in another town?* No one wanted the freak in their town, and because Hinchcliff Estate Agents being the only one in town due to the towns size well... *She should have got the hint, no house, no home, goodbye!*

And Tristan, her lovely, gullible, foolish Tristan. She had strung him along for years! She remembered the day that she realised he loved Kayella, he had invited her to the prom, and they had matching coloured items, so people knew they were a 'prom date couple'. They had become so close, he began to make the girl come out of her shell, she had even tried to stand up to Leanne, and that she would not allow.

Herself and Tristan being neighbours and their parents being good family friends made it easy for Leanne to manipulate the situation to her advantage. Plus, Tristan's family had money, she was used to money and wanted it to continue on for her married life too. She came up with a plan to come between Kayella and Tristan. She started knocking on daily round Tristan's house, being there when he got back from school or computer club. She started walking with him to school, she started asking him for homework help… Telling him how nice he looked, how his brains were impressive, how her parents adored him… How they should go to the prom together instead… She remembered the day of the prom, Tristan was meant to pick up Kayella in his dad's car, but Leanne's parents had ordered a Limo, it had arrived just before he was due to leave. She wore the prettiest damn dress known to man, almost like a prom come wedding dress, showing him what she could become, their future. She acted so excited, holding his hand, leading him to the Limo… Saying how excited her parents were, and how they couldn't let them down, it would be rude… So, they turned up to prom together… Kayella turning up half an hour or so late after walking there alone in her 'Charity' shop dress. The look on her face was priceless, the look on Tristan's guilty face as she danced with him, his arms wrapped around her and not the freak.

And yet now, somehow… He stood united with Kayella.

She shifted her head to look at them both more, but a sharp tugging pain pulled at her cheek and scalp. She had assumed the heavy feeling was just being damp from the bathroom which felt like a lifetime ago, or being hit around the head by something, but the feeling felt, sinister… Something was wrong!

She tried to turn to look, she could feel Jared beside her, but the pain and tearing sensation was too much to bear.

They had been glued, stuck together!

Bile rose in her throat, glue, like super glue. She could feel that it had hardened, parts were crusted, they were well and truly stuck and had been for a while.

"Jared", she whispered, her mouth pulling to one side as her lips had been partially glued to him.

A gentle murmur sounded out from beside her, but nothing tangible.

She could feel him beside her, his warmth, his aura and protection. She knew he would do what ever he could to protect her, to make sure no harm came to her. It was strange, she knew he loved her, and although Leanne was used to using other people, she knew that deep down she really and truly loved him back.

Judging by Tristan's presence, it wasn't just that he was aiding Kayella in her murderous killing spree, oh no. Him being there, kind and gentle Tristan being there, meant that he knew. He knew of her and Jared's affair and most probably knew of their plan to take his dads company for all they could and for her to marry Tristan and then divorce him a year or so down the line and take half the house and money. She, no they... would be rich beyond their dreams, and would have one of the biggest houses in town, people would see them and admire how far in life she had come, how far they had come. If she'd had a heart, she would have felt bad for leading Tristan on all these years. But her heart was cold as ice and all she cared and thought about was, the money...

"Jared, I need you", She whispered, "Please get me out of here, I'm scared".

Another inaudible mumble sounded from beside her.

"Jared? You, ok?" She asked, not really wanting to know the answer.

"Mm…mmm".

She couldn't turn her head to look, so she reached out her hand to feel his face. She traced her fingers along his lips, she felt the crusted dryness of the glue… The sick bitch had glued his mouth shut!

"AHHH", she shrieked in panic, she tried to move in a flash of blind panic. But pain, burning, tearing pain ripped through her face, scalp, arm and torse… The bitch had glued them together in so many places.

Footsteps echoed as Kayella sashayed over to them, her designer heels rubbing it in Leanne's face that she was doing alright… The designer was a brand Leanne had always adored and wanted but even she couldn't afford… Tristan must have told her to get them and wear them, just to annoy her, just to rub it in her face.

The footsteps stopped and Kayella leant down to where Leanne lay, shivering in pain. She leant ever closer to her ear and whispered, "Wakey, wakey".

Leanne snivelled, she could feel snot dribble out of her nose, and tears began to stream down her face.

"Oh no, have the crocodile tears entered the room?" Kayella teased.

Leanne couldn't help it, she blubbed, sobbing, huge emotional heaves of fear and pain, "Why? Why are you doing this?" but she knew, she already knew.

Kayella said nothing and stood up, she took a mic out of her cloak pocket and tapped a button. A static sound hissed from a nearby speaker and music began to play.

More sobs erupted from her, she knew that the music was Kayella's way to kill.

"I'm sorry".

Kayella had opened her mouth to sing but froze before a single lyric could pass her lips. She looked down at the girl that lay terrified on the floor, her eyes heavy with anger. She bent down quickly, a flash of angry speed, Leanne felt the air beside her face almost compress from it. "You don't get to be sorry".

"But I am, I'm so sorry the way I treated you", more tears and snot fell down her face.

"It changes nothing", Kayella snapped, "Being sorry does not change all what you did to me, all what you took from me".

"No, I know it doesn't… I just wanted you to know", Leanne sobbed harder, the movement pulling her and Jared, causing them both to writhe in pain.

"Should have glued your mouth shut too", Kayella hissed, then she motioned something to Tristan. He went to the side of the mirrored fun house, there seemed to be a laptop as she could hear a few clicks, like tapping of a keyboard, and then the song started again from the beginning.

Kayella lifted out another device from her cloak, it was two metal looking sticks, like what puppeteers use to control puppets, and at the end of one was a girl model and at the end of the other was a boy model. Leanne and Jared.

Death's Carousel

Leanne looked down at her hands, a rope with ribbons had been tied to them both, they were her puppets.

"Kayella please, please I'm sorry, really sorry. Please stop, don't do this... please".

Kayella looked angry, in fact she looked beyond angry, a sodden madness had taken over her eyes, "Remember when I begged you to stop? When I asked you to stop pulling my hair, to stop putting glue and pins on my chair, to stop making lies and rumours about me, to stop kicking and punching me, to stop hurting me, to stop taking pictures of me and editing them so I looked naked and plastering them all around the school. Did you stop?"

Leanne shook her head, skin and flesh tearing, blood pooling under her cheek, "No, I didn't".

"Exactly, then why should I?"

"Because your better than me, a better person, a better soul than me... Please".

"Don't use your Psychology crap on me...What about when you covered my hand in glue on a trolley and a nail tech had to acetone me off, or when you glued a mirror in the girl's bathroom and then pushed my face on it and the same nail tech had to come with the fire brigade to free me! Did you ever think I was a nice person then and that you should stop?" Kayella sounded furious.

"That wasn't just me..."

"I know, why do you think Jared is beside you, why do you think all the others were here, why do you think they are all dead?" she hissed.

Leanne felt a wave of guilt wash over her, all those years she tormented this girl and now it all led to this. She had to try another tactic, trying to reach to Kayella's good side was not working, her good soul had diminished, it was gone, extinguished like a candle's flame.

"Please don't do this, my, my face hurts already", Leanne cried.

"Oh, your face hurts. Well now you will know how it feels. After you glued my face to a mirror my skin got worse, I had to wear suncream even in the winter because the chemicals had burnt my skin, made it super sensitive to UV rays and sunlight, especially after being burnt by a chemical toilet and then fucking glue!"

Leanne trembled, she knew she had done so much wrong to Kayella, treated her worse than shit she had trodden in on her shoe, "No, that's not true, you had to wear the sunscreen because of Marielle, because of what she did to you at her home!"

Kayella's face thundered over, "Yeah that's right, just a prank, as always, but you putting more chemicals on my already over chemically processed face made it worse! You cannot just blame her, you burnt me too," She turned away and got ready once again for her performance.

The music played and Kayella sung and lifted the puppets up.

"Your skin looks fine now though, so it couldn't have damaged you that bad!" Leanne sniped, but she immediately regretted it.

Kayella stomped over and pulled out a tube of super glue from her cloak pocket. Leanne began to wriggle and writhe, Jared moaned in pain from her reaction. Kayella grabbed her head in a vice like grip, uncrewed the tube with her teeth and spat it out to the floor, the plastic lip rolled lazily to Leanne's shoulder. Her fingers pursed Leanne's lips together as she poured the glue over her mouth, she rubbed them together until the glue turned tacky and crystalising, the skin starting to tear. She let her head go with a fierce push, "I had to have plastic surgery, Botox and Hyaluronic acid injections to save my face. The chemical burns reduced the collagen I had in my skin, it deteriorated, even now I have to have top up injections to stop my skin from sagging and peeling. So yeah, you couldn't have damaged it that bad, could you? Now shut your goddamn face!"

Leanne rolled back, her skin pulling against Jared's. Small moans emitted from him, but Leanne was numb. The tears and snot from her cry-baby, crocodile tears had semi blocked her nose, and she felt the lack of air make her feel woozy and dizzy.

Kayella walked back to her stage, and lifted the puppets, her eyes burning into Leanne's, "Punch and Judy their strung, puppets for the puppeteer on string, a professor, a teacher of violence… No need to take offence… getting high on glue, till their lips turn blue, putting pins on seats, till my blood runs true, their laughter-like voices of a kazoo, Ooo…"

She lifted the puppets up higher, till it looked like they were standing… Then she turned to Tristan who turned a wheel of a cog that had been set up by the door of the house of mirrors. A mechanical whirr sounded out and the ropes that held her hands began to lift. The rope pulled and lifted, forcing her to her feet. Jared's ropes didn't move but being glued to Leanne forced him to stand, so as not to rip in half he scrambled quickly, his mouth unable to scream out in pain.

Leanne felt her body sweat, a hot flush of guilt.

"Judy peels glue from her face... Stuck together, outlines to trace... Punch peels glue from his face... Stuck together, outlines to trace..."

Another movement of Kayella's wrist and the puppets danced, the huge cog turned, and Leanne twirled as if dancing. Jared caught on quickly and moved with her body. It still pulled and pain tugged at her skin, but it wasn't as bad as before.

Kayella smiled wickedly, her amusement at Jared's quick thinking becoming a game. She twisted the puppets, gyrated them in the air, making more difficult and unattainable moves. She laughed as Jared tried and failed to keep up, not being able to breathe properly, not getting enough oxygen to keep up, and then skin and flesh ripping apart. Hearing Leanne's muted screams, and Jared hum through his un-opening mouth.

"Bikini photos from the beach, edited so people can leech, stuck to the school with glue, I will never live this through, I'm not a prude, but damn girl they look nude, and now everyone is being so rude, even the teachers, now being leech-ers, my bodies a pin up, a seaside cone cup, Punch wants to lick me, Judy wants to kick me..."

The song changed tempo as many of Kayella's songs did, it got faster, which meant the dance movements became quicker and more vigorous. She twirled the sticks fiercer, making the movement more demanding, Tristan turning the cogs, to mimic the exact movement. Leanne could hear her skin being torn, she felt hot, sticky warmth flow down between her and Jared. The imagery was not lost on her.

Death's Carousel

"Punch me and kick me, Judy…Judy does hate me, my pictures are scattered, with pins and glue, now back to you…"

A click of a button on her mic and a tub that hung from the ceiling tipped, hundreds of pins tinged to the floor. The metallic tings grinding on Leanne's nerves. Some got caught between the two of them, between the parts where their bodies became one. They pinched in, stabbing into their sensitive skin, like hundreds of tiny knives.

Kayella flicked her puppeted wrist again, and Leanne moved, but Jared, tiring and struggling for air stumbled and fell. The fall pulled harshly on them both, Leanne pulled on the ropes to fall with him but not quick enough. Hot flashes of pain rippled through her as his arm tore away from her. She screamed inside her closed mouth, the skin tearing, trying to make a new mouth for her to scream from, she writhed in horrific pain as her flesh peeled away and sat on its new host. Blood and muscle could be seen, the blood bubbling and oozing.

"Judy peels glue from her face, Stuck together, outlines to trace, Punch peels glue from his face, Stuck together, outlines to trace…"

An image filled Leanne's mind as dark spots and stars threatened to pass her out. She hung in limbo, her mind present but past…

* * *

The screams of pain echoed down the school corridor, crowds of kids lined the hall trying to catch a glimpse, or hear the pain being inflicted on the freak.

The scream, pained howls of a banshee as Kayella was slowly peeled off from the mirror in the girl's bathroom. Hot tears flushed down her cheeks, the patch where the glue stuck was hot, irritated and sore.

Leanne howled with laughter on the floor of the corridor, hidden by a group of students from the year below. The teachers all knew Leanne played pranks on the freaky girl, but the stupid girl never grassed her up, so Leanne just kept getting away with it. This one had to be her best yet!

Nancy and Sinead came towards her, they too had eyes full of tears of laughter.

"We did it, the photos are all up!"

She grinned from ear to ear, all they had to do was wait.

Eventually the poor freak was released from her own reflection, it must have been hard staring at your skanky self for hours.

The medical officer lead her out of the toilet. Her cheek red raw and swollen. She stopped and paused, looking at something on the wall opposite the toilet. A photo blown up, of her... naked! She hadn't been naked, not for the photo, she had worn a bikini down the beach, but it had been edited out... Kayella reeled in shock, not only was she in pain and embarrassed, but no, it was never enough, of course there was more! There was always more!

"Who is responsible for this?" The medical teacher shouted, "Come on, show yourself. Your so big and brave to do it behind our backs... Come show yourself, let's see if your still big and brave then!"

Death's Carousel

Of course, Leanne and the others stayed quiet, pretending to be shocked like the others, trying to stifle their giggles.

Kayella caught Leanne's eye and shot her a look. For a split-second Leanne almost felt slight remorse, but then it was gone, as if her brain never processed remorse as a real feeling. She just smiled, a big grin from ear to ear.

Ouch… Pain…So…Much…Pain…

*   *   *

Leanne came back to the present, her eyes swimming with black spots from the unyielding pain that racked her whole being.

She had been moved by the rope and Jared had tried to lift her in her fainting episode, but in doing so had ripped his torso away from hers, they were now only joined by their cheeks, entwined together as one, as conjoined twin flames. The pain was immense, like nothing she had ever felt before.

"The puppeteer now moves you, you dance to my tune, in the theatre box, I pull the strings, and close the locks, I stuck you together, in hell you both belong, as you dance to my deathly song… The glue shall pair, making you as one, my revenge has only just begun, and now it seems I have won… Punch wants to lick me, Judy wants to kick me…"

Leanne peered up at Kayella, her nauseated body tired, and aching from the night's events. She could tell the end of the song was nigh, and the end was near for her and Jared.

Kayella pulled the arms of the puppet up, "You say I'm crazy, you wouldn't be wrong..." She pulled the puppets further apart, "I wasn't born a bitch, people like you made me itch..." Then with a whip of her hand Kayella threw one puppet to the side of the room, it landed with a thump, crumpled up hitting a wall and then sliding down.

Realisation hit her and Jared instantaneously and they hugged and held each other for dear life. Leanne sobbed into Jared's shoulder, she bit and tore at the glue on her mouth, making a tiny hole, she breathed in a small amount of air and then tried to breathlessly say, "I'm sorry, I'm so sorry", but only muted hissing noises sounded out.

He couldn't reply, but she felt his warmth, felt comforted, his arms enveloping her, not wanting to ever let go, and even though she couldn't speak properly, he knew, he knew how sorry she was...

The mechanical whirr of the cog turning, the ropes pully being pulled then... WHOOSH! Jared was up in the air and flying, Leanne hadn't noticed another rope holding her down in place like an anchor, being held tightly in place as Jared left her for a final time.

As his body flew, she stayed put, Kayella holding on to the rope for dear life, not even faltering as the rope pulled hard, black leather gloves had been worn in readiness for the rope burn that would come, her grip deathly strong, superhuman strong, the revenge and pure hatred made her strength tenfold.

Death's Carousel

His body impacted against the wall and dropped to the floor in a crumpled pile of bloody flesh and broken bone. He screamed out in pain, his lips tearing apart, ripping open in a gush of blood and gargled cries.

The pain didn't hit Leanne at first and she stood there looking at Jared's broken body, her own feeling deathly numb. Then she realised what Jared being torn from her meant. Pain fluctuated across her face. She lifted a hand to feel her face, only to realise some of it was no longer there. Touching her mouth, or where her lips should have been all she could feel was her teeth. She could no longer close her mouth properly and red dribble and saliva dripped down her chin, down her top and pooled on the floor around her feet.

"I say your crazy too, cause you started this, but I'm the crazy bitch, that will finish this…"

Her hollow words echoed around her, like the orbs and flashes of pain that swayed like a boat on rocky waves. She held onto her mashed-up face, her hand holding onto the hot, sticky, wetness that was once her mouth.

"Judy peels glue from her face, Stuck together, outlines to trace, Punch peels glue from his face, Stuck together, outlines to trace…"

The song ended and Kayella dropped the puppet to the floor. Tristan dropped the rope that held Leanne connected to the rope. She dropped to her knees, the wetness of her bloodied drool seeping into her knees. She held the rope that held her hands together and she pulled at them mindlessly. They hadn't even been tied that tightly, she could have released herself before if she had just tried when they were lying on the floor at the start… *She could have got out? They could have got out? She could have not had her face torn off? Was that some sort of sick joke! Was that the prank, the final prank for her?*

Rage filled her body, freedom had been attainable. She could have just wriggled a bit more and undone the ropes, but her weight, gravity and the pully system kept it tight enough for the show, she just hadn't even bothered to try and escape... She was a fool!

She stood up, Kayella looking at her. No shock in her eyes at the girl's sudden movement, just a mere amusement that glowed from her dark, piercing eyes.

She glanced at Jared's lifeless form, his crumpled dead body. His scream had been his last breath. She let out a howl of pain, pain from her body and pain from her heart breaking... And then she ran...

Chapter Seven ... House of Shards ...

Leanne ran, her legs pumping, her arms cruising in the air steadying her as she wobbled from the blood loss and adrenaline. Blood poured from her face as the rise in blood pressure caused it to gush from her smile-less lips.

The house of mirrors was the closest building to her, and she had no choice but to aim for it, to hope that she could hide in there and lose Kayella and Tristan.

Her footsteps pounded on the metal steps that led up and into the building. The lights must have been on some form of sensor as they burst on as she collided into the first mirror out of disorientation and blindness from the flashing rainbow that danced before her eyes. The mirror wobbled with the impact as she fell to the floor. Nausea threatened her gullet, but fear made her crawl to her feet and again she moved.

Glancing in the mirror she saw Kayella making her way to the mirrored fun house. Her cloak billowing out around her like some form of dark entity.

Panic spurred her on and she threw her hands out to feel her way, not trusting her vision to distinguish between mirror and walkway.

Her pulse quickened as she made it around a few of the mirrored bends, her hands tracing the cool wobbling glass. Her face looked distorted, elongated and lip-less, blood streaming and her white teeth frozen in a forever smile. She looked like a monster from a horror story, like a mutated zombie that had bitten into another for a meal, strings of bloodied drool ran down her chin and blossoming down her shirt. She felt tears, hot, steaming tears roll down her cheeks at the sight of herself. *Had she really been nasty enough to deserve this?*

Footsteps danced delicately behind her as Kayella started the chase. Leanne swung her head round to spot where the killer-ess was standing, but the mirrors reflected the nightmare all around her, she couldn't tell what was mirror and what was the real murderer.

She let out a strangled cry as she carried on, feeling, moving, footsteps shuffling.

SMASH!!!

She screamed in terror as one of the mirrors shattered behind her, the maze of mirrors slowly becoming one solid path for the predator to find their prey.

Looking back briefly she spotted Kayella wielding the 'Whack a mole' hammer she had used on Leanne before like it was a sword, she swiped it left to right, shattering everything glass in her path. She seemed unfazed at the shards of mirrored glass that flowed in the air around her. Her dark cloak and hair swallowing up the shards, they lay gently on her hair as if they were expensive diamonds, glistening in the flashing rainbow lights.

CRUNCH, CRUNCH, CRUNCH!!!

Kayella's footsteps crunched over the shattered mirrored remains as she made herself ever closer to Leanne's position.

Leanne spun and tried to run again, no longer trying to feel her way, she just ran. She flitted round one corner, then bounced into a mirrored wall, turning she ran to another bobbling version of herself, then charging to the next she was weaving through the maze of glass.

SMASH, SMASH, SMASH!!! The noise of terror carried on echoing behind her. The tinkling of broken glass rushing around her like a demonic waterfall.

WHOOSH! SMASH! The air rippled beside her.

Leanne stopped, stunned… The hammer was embedded in the mirror that stood in front of her. Cautiously she turned and came face to face with Kayella, her time was up, there was no place to run anymore.

She shook with fear, her eyes darting around, looking at everything and nothing. She held her hands up in a surrender and knelt down on her knees.

Kayella stopped before her, her delicate frame menacing, Leanne could feel and taste the violence coming off her in waves, like iron and shit.

"Sorry", she whispered again, even though she knew it was fruitless, there would be no forgiving from the girl she had tormented for an eternity.

Kayella knelt beside her and grabbed a fistful of hair in her hand. Leanne screamed out in pain and fear, her heart hammering in her chest, fresh doses of blood pouring from her wound. She could feel dizziness come to take her, but her mind held on, hoping for a way out.

"Why are you sorry Leanne?" Her voice sounded soothing, innocent, the change from immense violence to immense innocence threw Leanne off, confused her.

"I'm sorry, for doing this to you… For doing this to everyone… I made a huge mistake", sobs wracked her body, her voice strange from the lack of lips to pronounce proper words, "I didn't mean for people to get hurt and die… I didn't mean to push you to the limit, we can get you help Kayella, I can get you help… I'm just so sorry my actions turned you into this… monster! You used to be such a quiet, innocent girl…and…"

Kayella stopped her, "Don't try to take the moral high ground, pretending to want to help to save your own vile skin. Yes, you did this, but I will finish it".

Leanne looked at her with pleading eyes, but it was too late.

Kayella opened her mouth, but not to say something, but to sing, one last song. There was no background music playing this time, she was singing a song on the spot, her creative mind flowing with imaginative horror juices, "Mirror, mirror, who's the sharpest of them all?".

Leanne's remains of her mouth trembled, her teeth chattering together, if she had still had her lips they would have trembled too, but they were stuck to Jared, like some glorified parting gift.

Death's Carousel

"Think I just remembered something, the mirror reflected it to me, like a clear looking glass, a river of memories, a crystal ball, who is the fairest of them all?"

Kayella used her strength to drag Leanne across the floor, shards of glass shredded into her legs and knees, like a thousand bee's all stinging and stabbing her at once.

"I look into the mirror, I quiver, at the person I see right now, it shatters all over the floor, oh no, it smashes, oh well, seven years bad luck don't seem swell, who's the sharpest of them all?"

Her sweet melodic voice pulled Leanne into a semi coma like trance, she felt her body relax, felt her mind give way to what would come.

"I see the reflection of me, she's been couped up, she wishes to be free, mirror, mirror, mirror of me, I see the reflection of you, and everything you put me through, mirror, mirror, mirror of you…"

Time slowed down leaving Leanne reeling and the hallucinations began… The glass all around her slowly raised up from the ground it had settled on, it floated around, swirling like a mixture of magical orbs. The shards turned to show the mirrored side, she saw her reflection in them, how distorted, cracked and broken she was, and not just physically.

Life events played out like small home movies on each pointed broken shard, everything she had done wrong, everything she had done to cause trauma to a human being that hadn't deserved it.

Blood poured from hands at a sweet sixteenth, sewing needles flitted over the wounds but then they snapped, shattering… blue liquid pulsated from a pair of eyes that stared at her, they cried the chemical induced liquid, leaving trails of burn marks as they dripped... A bloodied mouth, a tongue licking the blood, it dripping down creating a syrupy look, white teeth smiling out from beneath the ruby red liquid... Sharp shards of pins littering a seat, they grew bigger and bigger, the points becoming elongated like shafts of swords, blood dripping down each one... On each sword was a head, Nancy, Marielle, Mario, Sinead, Luke and her Jared, her beloved Jared... But one was free and waiting for its head... hers! Flames ripped through melting the silver of the swords, pooling into a mirror, a looking glass... Skin was etched onto the frame, skin that had been glued in place, the skin rolled and turned, eyes and teeth growing from within... Rolling to look at her and screaming... More images flooded her mind, hair pulling, hair cutting, pinching, kicking, rancid food, whispers from the past... Finally... Finally, the images slowed down... They were moving up and down, almost like a ride, carnival music blared out, in tune with the rise and fall...

The Carousel! Lights blinked and flashed all around, the ghosts of the fallen swirling in a mist of screams and pain, their soulless eyes glued to the ride that spun in a motion of endlessness.

Leanne opened her eyes to see she was now inside the mirrored glass column that resided in the centre of the Carousel. The horses rising and falling, their decaying eyes glaring into the glass prison.

"I think our world is crumbling, I think I'm spiralling and tumbling, down a giant rabbit hole, through a mirrored void, I fall... I wish I could stand and be tall... But the mirror image of me is cracking up..."

A sprinkling noise sounded from above, as if hundreds of shards of glass had been let loose in the roof of the carousel, spinning and shattering, cascading trying to find a way out.

"I look into the mirror, I quiver, at the person I see right now, it shatters all over the floor, oh no, it smashed, oh well, seven years bad luck don't seem too swell, who's the sharpest of them all?"

The trinkling of glass became louder and louder, it was getting closer and closer. The lights flashing around the spinning machine... Leanne felt numb as she saw each and everyone of her friends splattered to a horse. Nancy's gaping hole in the head to her spine, a clear view to hell...

Sinead, her fried and drowned remains dripping on the horse that melted with her... Marielle, blue, her face frozen in the chemicals that burned her inside and out, that drowned her sorrows, the horse merging with her, turning blue with every rotation... Mario, his caved in head resting against the golden pole that held him in place, shattered teeth and shards of skull flicking out into the wind with each turn, being pulled out by gravity... Luke... Burnt to a crisp, his body toasted and twisted on the horse, a rocket launcher stuck to his side, almost as if it had melted to him... whisps of gentle smoke wafting off his body as it still cooled from the burning heat of hell that consumed him... Jared... her Jared... His flesh ripped and open like large open sores, muscle and bone revealing the person inside... Extra bits of flesh flapped in the wind as the carousel spun... Those bits of flesh her own... They called to her in a hypnotic display of gore.

"I see the reflection of me, she's been couped up, she wishes to be free, mirror... mirror...mirror of me... I see the reflection of you, and everything you put me through... mirror, mirror, mirror of ... You".

The clattering and shattering noise of death grew louder, louder and louder... A droplet of glass fell to her shoulder, a stabbing pain as it sliced down, gravity pulling it hard.

"I see the reflection of me, she's been couped up, she wishes to be free..."

A few more shards flittered down, dusting her face in a shard tirade of pain, like a tirade of verbal abuse but coming in the form of a thousand tiny glass knives.

"Mirror, mirror, mirror of me..."

The top of the carousel had been turned into a funnel shape, the funnel leading out to where the column resided, where Leanne stood awaiting her fate.

"I see the reflection of you... And everything you put me through..."

A few more large shards sliced down from the funnelled hole in the ceiling, one grazed her face, slicing a massive line, her face flapping open, blood spewing out... But she felt nothing, she was numb...

"Mirror, mirror, mirror... of... You!"

With the last word, thousands of shards of glass tumbled down from the ceiling. They bit into her flesh, tore at her skin, penetrated her body and mind. Leanne looked out to where her friends lay dead... The rain of glass

Death's Carousel

slicing her into hundreds of tiny fleshy pieces… Then nothing… Just silence…

Chapter Eight ... Prom Date Fate...

Cheesy music blared out from the school auditorium, the hall vibrating with the throng of students dancing and celebrating their last weeks at the school, before moving on and up into the adult world.

Kayella stood at the front door of the hall, the colourful lights shining over her like some sickly aura. Balloons billowed out around her feet as she gingerly took a few steps into the room.

She looked at everyone around her, smiles on all their faces as they danced with their friends, their boyfriends, their girlfriends, even the teachers danced in the corners, secretly watching the students like hawks to make sure no contraband had been smuggled in to spike to punch bowl.

The song that played called to her, "You don't love her, oh you belong to me, You don't love her, I'm here waiting, set me free…"

Death's Carousel

She felt pain and upset wrack her body as she spotted him, he stood there in the suit they had chosen together, with his colourful pocket filler to match her dress. But instead of being with her, he was with Leanne, and she had the same colour dress as her, to match with him too.

Had this been their plan all along? To get her to fall for him, to humiliate her? To make her feel loved, to make her feel like she had someone and then to take it all away?

Kayella had waited, waited for half an hour for him to collect her in his dad's car, but he never showed, he stood her up as if she was worthless. Her nan had forgotten it was prom, laughed at her for dressing up, saying that the wedding for her mum wasn't until next week, her mum... of course, was dead. Her mind and brain failing her, she had no one to confide in, no one to pour out to, to tell them how upset she was, how life had given her another unfair blow.

As they danced Leanne turned and spotted her, a sly grin washed over her face as she pulled Tristan in closer, made him hold her waist as she leant her head on his shoulder.

Rage filled Kayella, a hormonal blind rage that was red, pure red and it glowed, glowed from inside. She walked over to him.

"You stood me up!" She snapped as he turned in the dance to face her.

His face fell in pain, not physical but emotional, "Kayella... I... Leanne's parents they... I couldn't say no... My mum... My dad... Said I'd be rude... I..."

"Forgot it, your just like her, just like them", and she motioned to Leanne and then to her little group of cronies that crowded round them.

His eyes broke, he knew he was becoming like them, he had crossed the line, but he loved her, he loved Kayella so much, but...

*

He was ready and waiting, his mum polishing his suit with her hands, dusting off any bits of flick.

"You look so handsome, so grown up", she smiled a warm, loving smile, "Make sure you look after that girl, I think she will be a keeper".

"Mum..."

"I mean it", she looked into his eyes, "She's sweet".

Then his dad appeared, and handed him the car keys, "Go get her soldier".

Tristan beamed from ear to ear. He took one last look in the hallway mirror, his suit was the one they had chosen together, her dress chosen to match his suit. He went to the door, pulled the handle and... Leanne!

"Oh, hi Leanne", his mum smiled but looking a little confused and uncomfortable.

"You ready T?" Leanne smiled, she looked beautiful, almost angelic. Her caramel blonde hair half up and half down and curled. Her makeup subtly pretty, her dress a mint green, matching his suit pocket, it hung off the shoulders showing off her cleavage, a large slit ran up the skirt revealing her long, toned legs.

Death's Carousel

"Er…" Tristan paused, "I… I'm taking Kayella… You know that".

Leanne's face dropped, "Oh… But I thought… that… Oh".

"Hi Mr and Mrs Hinchcliffe", Leanne's mum gasped from behind Leanne, "Oh my, don't they look adorable together. Well, the limo is here ready to take you both, and it's grabbing the others on the way".

He turned to look at his parents, they and Leanne's parents were good friends, Leanne's dad had even helped his dad get an investment to open up his own Estate Agents… The other one in town had been run by an older man who planned on retiring.

"Best not be rude Tristan", his dad said taking the keys from his fingers.

"But what about K…"

"I'm sure she will forgive you and meet you there", his mum whispered in his ear, "Just go along with it for now".

"No… No, I can't let her down", he said.

"Look, we can't risk upsetting them, we owe them money and they could make things… Difficult", his dad mouthed.

Tristan looked at Leanne, a look in her eye he couldn't quite read reverberated from them, "Ok".

Leanne squealed with joy, "Come, the limo has drinks and sweets and a camera that can print instant photo's".

Leanne's mum beamed with pride as the pair excitedly made their way into the rented Limo. Tristan's *mum and dad looked on with sombre expressions… If only they knew…*

*

"Kayella, I…", He tried.

"Save your apologies, you will all live to regret the fact that you all keep ruining my life. I will make you all pay!"

"Er, ok freak", Sinead giggled from beside Leanne.

"Like to see you try freak", Nancy retorted.

"Do you need me to escort her out", Mario boomed from beside them all, flexing his muscular frame.

Kayella just looked at them all, memorising all of their faces, their smiling, evil faces. Every freckle, every line, every eye lash was printed onto her brain, in her memories. She would get them all one day, she would be picked on no more.

As she spun on her heel, she didn't see the longing looks from both Tristan and Luke. Luke's heart was broken as she stormed out the hall, but he couldn't go to her, couldn't offer to be her date, they would all attack him.

"One day baby, one day I will be with you", he whispered menacingly.

On the other side of the room, with the music still thumping and the group of cackling witches not paying him any attention as they gossiped about the freaky girl Tristan looked on longingly, "I'm so sorry", he whispered, his heart shattering into a thousand pieces. And as Leanne took his arm, and danced joyously with him all night, he became numb…

Death's Carousel

*

Kayella closed her eyes, took a deep breath in and then let it out slowly, her body trembled with accomplishment and memories… It was done, she had taken revenge on all of those that had wronged her. Relief flooded through her, she felt at ease, calm, spiritually awakened, like nothing could bring her down from this unbelievable high.

TRISTAN!

He stood there, his eyes open but not really seeing. He stared into the glass column that housed his ex-fiancé. His lips trembled like Kayella's body had, but his was not of relief, or happiness or even accomplishment. It was of horror, pure horror at what they had achieved…

"Tristan?" She asked nothing in particular as she called his name, but the word asked so much all the same.

He turned to her, "I… I can't believe it's done", his voice quivered in the cool night air. Morning was approaching, the smoke from the fire at the bumper car ride was steadily taking over the rest of the fun fair compound, blending into the pink morning sky that blossomed like the petals of a cherry blossom tree or the blood that seeped down blonde hair, turning it pink, depending on how you looked at it.

The smoke would sure enough garner attention in the day light, that was if the flames flickering upon the night sky hadn't already.

"Yes", she replied, "It is done, and now we must leave, make sure there are no loose ends".

He looked at her, his face numb, "Yes, no loose ends".

"Then let's get to work", she said softly.

He didn't move right away, so she gently tapped him on the shoulder, he jumped, as if scared of her, she could almost taste his fear, it was intoxicating.

She smiled, amused, "Are you scared of me Tristan?"

He gulped but said nothing.

"We did this together… You and me…" she accused softly.

He licked his lips, "I know, I just… Leanne", he motioned to where she sat, sliced like ham in a packet from the supermarket.

"What?" Kayella shrugged confused, "You knew she had to die!"

"I know… Just… Like that? We agreed she would die but, it wasn't meant to be that way. It was meant to be quick and…"

"Well, she caused me years of pain, so I felt like prolonging hers for while", Kayella said cheerfully.

He looked at her, "We did something really bad… Don't you feel any remorse? Anything?"

She shook her head, "No… They felt no remorse when they tormented me, attacked me, cut me, murdered my soul and my sanity. So why should I?"

He stood there, his gaze glassing over.

"Are you with me?" Kayella asked him.

Nothing.

"Tristan are you with me or not?" she asked him, more firmly this time.

Death's Carousel

"Yes, yes of course", he said snapping back to the realm they were in,

She smiled, but it didn't reach her eyes, "Then let's make good".

As he turned to start the cleanup to hide any evidence of them, she knew he was a loose end.

He grabbed the petrol can that had been hidden under some rubble, he swashed the fuel around the premises, making sure to soak everything they had touched.

Kayella walked off to their 'control' room, she tapped a few keys on the keyboard. She watched back the footage that Tristan had captured of all her performances, none showed her face, some showed the outline of her body, but the lighting that had been used made glimpses of her hair look caramel blonde… *She could pass for Leanne*, she thought.

The rest of the footage showed only what they wanted the authorities to see, what she wanted them to see, if they saw it…maybe the fire would destroy it all, but if not, she wanted nothing coming back to her. She wanted that bitch to get all the blame… All of it!

Then… Kayella took her phone and connected it to the laptop, it was a burner phone but had footage and images that she had taken and edited to incriminate. She uploaded the documents she desired and then took a step back. She scanned through it all, still nothing to suggest she had ever been involved but everything she desired to be there, now was.

The door clicked open and in walked Tristan.

"The place is burning nicely, we should le…" he trailed off as he spotted the newest addition to the show…

He stood in full view of the camera throwing fuel to the fire, then lighting the match that fell to the floor and ignited...

"What? We agreed... I! I turned that camera off... There is nothing to..." Confusion, anger and regret flooded through him.

"Betrayal hurts doesn't it, Tristan", Kayella said, her voice calm, collected and strong.

"But I done as you said, I done all what was agreed!"

"Yes, but I can see the regret in your eyes, you don't feel the same about me anymore and I can't trust that you won't crumble and out me", she replied.

"No, no I would never, if I out you, then I would be outing myself", he started.

She held up a hand to stop him, "But I know I cannot trust you Tristan". She turned to look at the screen, the image frozen of him, "You see, you only wanted revenge for what Jared and Leanne did to you, what they did behind your back... You gave me the waffle of you always loving me, that you were a fool to have gone with Leanne, that she brainwashed you... Once upon a time, me and you could have been, we could have had something special, you and your parents always regrated the day you betrayed me for Lee... but... You had your dick inside her", she spat the last bit, like the words brought her a vile taste to her mouth, "You were going to marry her! And you never thought of me, not once, not until she screwed you!"

"I..." again she cut him off.

"You said you loved me, and I trusted you all those years ago. We agreed to go to prom together... we chose matching accessories for our outfits, I paid for your ticket to show you I meant how I felt about you, which was a big deal for me then. But you stood me up for her... I stood there waiting for ages... that knot of excitement turning into a knot of pain... I had been rejected once again. And when I decided to try and find you, well, you turn up in a Limo, you take her in, hand in hand straight to the dance floor... Then from then on you become a couple and buy a home together, sleep together, plan to marry one another... And now... Because she betrayed you and you hurt, you came to me, and we made plans... this was all as much you as it was me".

"I never meant to hurt you all those years ago Kayella", he whispered, "I was fooled into it, brainwashed by her, her family and mine... They wanted a union of money".

"And they nearly got it... But not anymore", she mused. She jumped up and spun on her heel.

Her sudden movement made him jump, although he was a man, a fully grown man, she scared him deep into his soul. The last song, the mirrors, none of that was planned, she had made that up on the spot. Her beautiful and dangerous mind creating something from nothing... Obviously she had planned the shards to funnel in the carousel, she had taken time to create that alone, without his knowledge and it was sickening. Powerfully sickening that her mind could conjure that with no help.

"So, what do we do now?" He asked, afraid of the answer she might provide.

She said nothing but stalked on over to him. He stood his ground not wanting to aggravate her in any way, she had clearly gone into full primal mode, she was beyond her childhood trauma now, she was the trauma.

She stopped right next to him, her body mirroring his, so close he could feel the heat from her skin, feel her breathing, "I... I can trust you right? We promise, to not out one another, to not crumble, to not judge each other for what we did here".

He glanced over at the screen, "But? The evidence you planted."

"I can wipe it, it's for insurance, I always keep receipts. You so much as whisper a word of this to anyone and that gets leaked, and you will be framed for it all. You are after all the computer genius in this. Everyone will think the scorned lover might have flipped and killed everyone in a moment of rage... But the poor little freaky girl... No one would suspect her... She's weedy, scared, fragile... You get my gist".

He nodded, "You have my word".

"Do I though?"

He nodded, "Yes, you do".

"Ok", she said calmly, her voice taking on a softer tone and she leant in for a hug, "No loose ends".

He hugged her back, "No loose ends", he breathed her in, her sweet berry scent, her anguish, her trauma, her pain, her triumph, her mental state and...

PAIN! Sharp breathtaking pain ripped through his back.

He took a weary step back from her and looked at her hand. A bloody shard of mirror with fabric wrapped around the handle end was covered in his blood. Confusion, fear and double-crossed betrayal thundered in the pain that rocked his body. "Why", was all his could whisper.

"Because I trust no one but me", she replied, "You would crumble and you would spill, I can see it in your eyes. The madness would drive you crazy until you spew it out… And I can't have that".

He fell to the floor, his knees buckling, he always thought in movies that if someone stabbed someone that they could fight back, that it was just a small wound, but the pain, blood loss, shock and potentially nerve damage made his body crumble.

"No loose ends", he whispered to her, looking away from her face, "That's what you meant".

She nodded, "Yes, you were the last loose end but not anymore".

"I hope you get the life you deserve", he sniffed, "I… I regret everything everyone did to you, but I don't blame you… I forgive you".

That hit Kayella in the heart, she had become so numb over the years, her walls build thick and strong, no one could penetrate them… But Tristan… She leant down to him, the mirrored shard she held clattering to the floor beside them.

"I wish it could have been different for us", she half smiled, a sadness filling her eyes.

Tristan leant towards her, his hands scrabbling for the bloodied shard. She watched him and didn't move. He wrapped his fingers around it and their eyes met.

She made no move to stop him, in fact she thought if this was meant to be then it was meant to be…

He lifted the shard, his hand holding on tight to the now bloodied handle. They looked at one another, no more words exchanged. He rose his hand and then brought it down hard…

Kayella closed her eyes and waited for the pain, a pain that didn't come. She opened her eyes to see the shard impaled into his stomach, then he took it out with a scream and then stabbed his back where she had driven it in, then again in his arm and leg.

"Why?" She asked confused, a panic flowing through her veins at his sudden madness.

"You need it… to…to… look like I did it… Like I committed all this…" his eyes fluttered as he tried to motion round the fair ground, "I need it to look like I did it… My hand killed them all, and… Myself. So hopefully you can forgive me, and so you can live on, a life that will make you happy".

A lone tear ran down her cheek, emotions had not been allowed to flow from her body in a long time… and even though a crack had appeared she only allowed one tear to break though, "I forgive you Tristan".

He let out a sigh of relief, "Then you best get going".

She looked around her, the fair ground was in full inferno, the flames edging towards them, their heat licking at her skin, her face felt warm.

Standing up and taking one last longing look at Tristan, one last look at what could have been, she headed to the hole in the fence where she had planned her exit.

Chapter Nine ... The Carousel Killers...

Smoke filled the air of the town as the raging fire tore through the old Riverside Fairground. Sirens sounded out as the fire brigade rushed to the scene. Floods of water pumping out to put out the smouldering rage, fire engines adding water from the Rivervalle lake behind the fair ground to speed up the process of putting all the smoking embers out.

Hours later all that was left was a smoking shell, hot patches still poured out with hissing smoke, but as it cooled down and the site was searched, the remains of the deathly carousel with melted and blackened dead bodies was discovered.

More sirens as the police called for backup, forensics arrived and began searching the rubble and debris.

One more body found, laying a few feet away, a sharp shard just a few centimetres away from an outstretched hand, scratched into the large shard was a delicate looking 'K'.

Detective Leon Kingston stood at the scene, leaning down to inspect the one lone body that wasn't attached to the fair ground ride like the others.

Sweat poured down his back as the plastic coverall encased him, heat was still emitting from the ruins causing his sweat to have sweat. He took notes and pictures of all what he could see, the forensics team also taking pictures and commenting on potential causes.

He studied the blackened mirrored glass shard as another officer on the scene approached.

"You think it's important?" The other officer asked, crouching down to peer at what he had found.

Leon shrugged, "Not sure, maybe? Could be from the Carousel, could be an old carving from when it was open and up and running, or maybe it was from others breaking in…"

"Or?"

"Or it could be a message", he replied studying the lone body, it was male but still charred although not to the extent of the other bodies. He spotted on one of his fingers, his pinky finger a diamond engagement ring, normally worn by a female fiancé although in these modern times that wasn't always the case. But the thing that struck him as odd was the prongs that normally encased the diamond and held it to the ring had been bent, the diamond taken out. It lay like a small glistening beacon just centre meters away.

Death's Carousel

"Did he cut the glass with the diamond?" The other officer asked.

Again, Leon shrugged, "Maybe it's a message for us, or for someone else, but yeah, I think he scratched the glass with the diamond".

"Wonder who the ring was for?" The officer asked grabbing evidence bags from their pocket and leaning down to pick them up after Leon had taken photos.

"His girlfriend? Maybe he planned to propose here, tonight, maybe it was some breaking and entering party that went wrong!" He said standing up and looking towards the Carousel. Other officers were finishing up there, so he decided to have another look now he wouldn't be in the way.

Just as he approached the melted carousel another officer approached, "Sir".

Leon looked at him, his lashes dripping from the heat, "Howards? Go on".

Officer Howards cleared his throat, "We just had a call at the station, we may have a potential witness as to what happened here. Or at least a tip off as to who done it".

Leon looked confused, "Really? A tip off already? But we haven't advertised it to the public yet".

"I know, but it seems someone got a call, a voice note from a friend, stating they may have accidentally killed people".

Leon sighed, "Right, I'm on my way". He took one last look at the probable murder scene and left.

*

Kayella sat in the air bnb she had rented purposely to have a cover story. It was run by a sweet little old lady who had security cameras all around the front of the property. But none to the side, where a convenient bathroom window sat.

She had a timer set which she had stolen from a hardware store, she didn't want those receipts, for the lights to make it look as if she was home. She had made sure the camera's saw her originally check in, then she had escaped through the bathroom window, leaving it open enough so she could shimmy it open on her return and just climb in. Piece of cake.

On her return she had showered, packed away her cloak that she had worn and hidden it in a secret compartment in her suitcase. Her plane ticket was booked for that day, she just had to set the wheels in motion to cover herself.

She pulled out her phone, she had left Leanne's phone in the inferno after using it one final time to add the finishing touches, made sure it would be melted to mulch, she had even gone as far as to duplicate everything, she needed her own phone for backup purposes and had kept it at the Air b n b so any timings and messages that may be looked into, she would have received here and not there. She was determined to cover her tracks. There would be nothing, nothing of course to incriminate herself, but to incriminate others! It had been a long-planned process, to hack all their phones, to plant messages. That once they kidnapped them to keep up pretences and to keep up the messaging and social posting. She checked the phone, more importantly her messages and smiled.

The conversation she and Leanne had before she finally died was voice recorded to Leanne's phone that Kayella had taken from her when they had drugged the group. She had edited it for her required purpose and then sent it as a voice note, a message to her own phone as a call for help from the fair ground… Sure enough it was a risk to take, but if the evidence piled up against Leanne and no one was there to fight her corner, then the hope was the police would not delve too much into it… Although if they did the location and timings would at least add up.

She picked up her own phone and opened the message, it was 7.08am, and she hoped that it would look like Kayella had just woken up to receive the message.

She listened as Leanne's voice played out into the room she sat in, morning light from the curtain fanned through, dust particles floated in the air as the dead girl's voice called out like a ghost, "I'm sorry, for doing this to you… For doing this to everyone… I made a huge mistake, I didn't mean for people to get hurt and die…" The memory of her lipless face, struggling to talk, to pronounce it all was vivid in her mind's eye, it made her smile. It was perfect, to someone else listening, it could just sound like someone who was having a murderous, emotional breakdown.

She held her phone close, listening to the nothingness that was around her. The quaint Air b n b was silent. As if everything was holding its breath… Then she dialled the emergency number, "Hi yes police please, yes I'll hold".

"Police, what's your emergency?" the operators calm voice asked from the other end.

She took a deep breath and then said, "I just received a weird message from an old school friend stating that she is sorry, she didn't mean for people to get hurt and die…"

*

The next few days became a blur, as expected she had to postpone her trip, but she did it willingly, making sure she was there to help with all investigations and questions. Luckily the record label was understanding and postponed their meeting by two weeks. But she didn't even need to wait the full fourteen days, within seven the police had decided that they no longer needed her, that if the detective or investigation team needed her, they would contact her or her agent, they decided that she was just as clueless as everyone else and that the case was pretty straight forward… A lover's tiff, Tristan had caught Leanne cheating weeks before the party and had found her plan to screw him over. Leanne by this point had already arranged a break and enter party at the old Riverside Fair ground and Tristan had turned it into a fun fair of horrors. A huge, weird game had played out which unfortunately turned into a mass murder of multiple friends that had unfortunately been at the wrong place at the wrong time.

Messages, emails and notes had been found by the police to prove everything. Multiple messages between Leanne and her friends, discussing the breaking and entering fun fair party, messages between Leanne and Jared hoping for Tristan to have an 'accident' at the party and then them being able to run off into the sunset together and take the money. All of which had been set up by Tristan and Kayella herself.

The skills Tristan had taught her and left her with were what made the deception possible and as she flew over the country on her way to her new life. She smiled warmly, revelling in what had been accomplished. She had got the best revenge, not served cold at all, but warm and it was fun… Revenge was all the fun at the fair.

Looking down over the veins of the world below her, pulsating with life, the humans were the blood of the world, their ignorance bliss, they kept it pumping and flowing. But what made it extra special was how the world was hers, she had it at her fingertips. She was about to embark on a new career, one that would make people adore her and love her, far, far away from the life she'd had before. Her revenge had taken away her haters, made them suffer like she had, and she knew new haters may rise from their ashes, but she had the power now, and her power could take down anyone and burn them all to the fucking ground! She would never be weak, EVER AGAIN!

Piper Nuelle

News Reports...

I-mmediate News... Rivervalle's number one stop for news.

'The Carousel Killers! A scorned lover and his wrath, a once paranoid computer engineer, and a cheating soon to be wife whose money ideals won the true affections of her heart... Those are the two suspects that also died, along with their victims, six others at the murder ground at 'The Riverside' Fun fair in Rivervalle. No other suspects are suspected at this time. It seems from evidence collected by the local police department that the first killer, a Miss Leanne McBride of Riverton Park a suburb in the town of Rivervalle, was the main instigator of the hideous crimes that were committed. She had lured six friends, 'nearly seven', to a party at her home address, before also arranging a breaking and entering party at the local disused fair ground that had been shut down some years ago when the owner's business went bust. The second killer a Mr Tristan Hinchcliffe also of Riverton Park was the fiancé of Miss McBride, he had a background in computer science and computer engineering and also had some home-self-taught hacking experience from evidence collected at the family home. It is believed that Mr Hinchcliffe hacked into the security system being used at the old fair ground and blacked out most of the camera's, blocking the sensors and then proceeded to film bizarre footage of each of the killings for the enjoyment of his fiancé, who police have said is seen walking around the crime scenes in a black cloak. They said it was something out of a horror movie with her roaming around like some sort of Grim Reaper, murdering her friends and then moving onto the next one.

It then seems that once all the victims were murdered the pair then turned on one another, Mr Hinchcliffe murdering his soon to be wife before then taking his own life due to discovering an affair between his soon to be wife and his best friend.

Drugs and alcohol were found at the home address, and in the systems of the victims that could be examined, although it cannot be conclusive for all victims and the two suspects due to the degree of burning and injuries done to the bodies.

The victims of the killers are;

Jared Knight, an estate agent who worked in Mr Hinchcliffe's family run estate agency, who is said to have been having an affair with Miss McBride, which officers have said from messages that it seems this caused tension between the two. It sent Miss McBride into a murderous psychosis and then Mr Hinchcliffe into a revenge murder of his fiancé and then the suicide of himself.

Sinead Wilson, a long time 'best friend' of Miss McBride according to character witnesses and an aspiring model and influencer.

Marielle Coppard and her brother **Mario Coppard**, both friends of both of the killers, although through messages it seems that there was some tension between them when Marielle had found out about the affair and had threatened Miss McBride with spilling the truth and some blackmail involvement.

Nancy Fairweather, another long-term friend of Miss McBride, although there seems to be some form of hidden relationship between McBride and Fairweather, although the full extent is unknown, but it seems the affair with the male was what pushed Tristan to murder and not her female affair.

Luke Godden, a friend of the group who also had a criminal record which doesn't relate to the case. But many have mentioned how their friendship circle seemed quite corrupt by very unstable individuals.

Reports have also come in of a survivor, another person was invited to the party but declined, it seemed to be due to work commitments and maybe even a distaste for the group. Their identity has not been confirmed as of yet although there are speculations as to whom…'

RiverValle Telegraph…

'The identity of the nearly seventh victim of the '*Carousel Killers*' has been revealed and named by the police and by her agent this morning.

Kayella Kennedy of Los Angeles CA has come forward as the survivor of the horrendous murders that rocked our small community, if she had been involved it would have taken the death toll to nine. As it stands the actual death toll is Eight including the two killers. She extends her deepest sympathies for all the families involved and affected by the crimes.

Death's Carousel

The once Rivervalle resident who has recently moved to Los Angeles to begin a career in the music industry admitted to receiving an invitation to a party of sorts from Leanne McBride. She had declined the offer of joining in with the doomed party, stating that a work commitment clashed with the timings, but that also due to the undesirable people present and being invited that she would most definitely not attend.

It is known to some about the horrific stalking incident Miss Kennedy encountered with Mr Godden back when she had just left school. But there has also been rumours of the group *'bullying'* Miss Kennedy at some point during their so called *'Friendship'*.

Miss Kennedy commented on that statement with, *'Most friendships fall apart at some point during schooling, and whilst I endured some not so happy memories, I would not like to talk bad of the dead, especially under these difficult and upsetting circumstances but my sincere thoughts go out to their families and all involved'*.

Although it seems that her *'Friends'* made some bad decisions and were at the wrong place at the wrong time, Kayella's life has taken a turn for the best, she is now putting Rivervalle on the map with being signed to a record label over in Los Angeles and is set to release a debut album later this year.

She added that her album will be dedicated to those that unfortunately lost their lives on that dreadful night…'

Piper Nuelle

Epilogue – Three Months Later...

"Let's welcome our musical guest tonight on Martina Talks, everyone let's give a round of applause for... Kayella... Kennedy!"

Screams, screams echoed all around her as she heard her name being called out by Martina 'Talks'. She actually couldn't believe it, this moment in time she was on a late-night talk show with one of the most popular talk show hosts Martina Schwartz. Her glam squad had glammed her up to the nines, she looked like she belonged in Hollywood. Her dark glossy hair poker straight and shining with health. Her makeup perfection, not a pimple or a flaw on show. Her dress was bubble-gum pink to show off her hot bod and playful persona, it hugged her waist and accentuated her boobs, then trailed down her legs before flowing out in a pool of silk and ribbons. It was a 'House of Sterling Steele', or 'HOSS' for short, a huge deal, a huge fashion brand, that had wanted to work with her... her shoes were also pink and had Rose Quartz crystals embedded into the fabric, they shone in the light and looked like pure magic.

Death's Carousel

The show runner stood at the side door, and as her name was called, the runner ushered her onto the stage through a pretend side door. Hot studio lights beamed down at her as she made her way out. She smiled a sultry smile and waved a perfectly manicured hand to the audience, all of which carried on screaming her name, some in tears, some reaching out to try and touch her aura as she passed.

She perched herself down onto a cute fluffy beige couch, the fake red brick backdrop behind her making her feel as if she was in a cute New York style apartment.

Martina Shwartz was a forty something middle aged woman who loved to work out, her incredibly toned body had a figure-hugging jump suit in black with sparkles littered over in segments. Her slim athletic legs crossed one another as she enthusiastically chattered away to her guest, her long blonde hair shimmered in the studio lighting.

"Welcome, welcome… Miss star of the moment, Kayella".

"Thanks for having me", Kayella practically beamed.

"So, how does it feel to be America's sweetheart of the moment?" Martina said, her long slender fingers wrapping around one another as she tried to look sophisticated.

"Totally unreal… But… Magical", she replied.

"Magical indeed! But what is also magical is your music style, please fill us in on how you make such horrifyingly depressing lyrics feel upbeat and catchy. I mean, what is it they call your style of music… Death pop?"

Kayella nodded and then spoke with her hands, "Yes, so Death pop in my music stems from the real emotions and experiences I have had throughout my life. My first debut album is actually about experiences that I felt but also... What my friends have gone through".

"Ah yes, it is known that your album named 'Carousel', is a dedication to your friends that died from the killings in your hometown", Martina said, "Now, some people love that you dedicated it to them, but some feel it is in bad taste, what would you say to those that, fail to grasp or understand your reasoning?"

"I come from a very small town, and not just me but everyone was affected by the murders. Yes, I had a narrow escape of being another victim, but I went to school with the victims, they were my friends, I also had other, not so friendly experiences with some of them and I just feel that it is reflected in my music. It has helped me process what happened to them, what happened to me and my home. I've had many people from my hometown express gratitude for my album and how it has helped them grieve, move on and accept what happened. I just feel that grief shouldn't be ignored, and we all have a voice, I just use mine to sing and express my inner minds conflict to help me heal. And all I want is for others to heal".

"Wow, that is such a powerful concept, I very much appreciate you sharing that with us. Hopefully now more of us can understand your grief", Martina said taking her hand and holding it with such sorrow and respect.

Kayella looked away, she feigned a foreign tear that gently stroked her cheek. She needed to look the part, to show emotion, to show grief... She wanted no one to suspect... No loose ends.

"I also have worked out with my label that a proceed of my earnings from the album and the coming tour will be donated to a charity set up in my hometown of Rivervalle to help the families and friends of the victims", Kayella said innocently.

The crowd went wild, applauding her generosity.

"Wow, that is... Amazing. So generous. See people, not all musical artists want all the money for themselves", Martina said, a few horrified gasps and a few glorified cheers echoed round the studio. Martina was known for being a little 'under the belt' with her words, but that was why people loved her, and she would make people love Kayella. Only the biggest stars got onto Martina Talks... Kayella was the first, lesser celebrity to appear, but that would all soon change.

The rest of the show went on without a hitch, she felt the adoration from the fans and all the crew from the show. Many commenting on how brave she was. Her social media also grew overnight. She was almost overwhelmed with how fast things were happening, by how fast her fan base was growing, people truly loved her.

She had pretty much made a deal with the devil to change her life, and he had, in more ways than she could have imagined. Life was finally good.

The after party was banging, the drinks flowing, the music pounding and the company exceptional. She was rubbing shoulders with the rich and famous, actors and actresses alike smiled at her or made small talk, other musical artists chatted to her, told her the tips of the trade and the who's who of the music world.

As the party came to a close, she noticed a police officer standing by the bar, he was clearly on duty and not drinking, but he had his eyes on her. She felt the hairs on the back of her neck rise, his glare was of someone trying to sus someone out. But his face, she knew that face…

She made her way to the bar, her heels clacking on the polished wood floor, her hips sashaying in her dress. She leant over and asked the bar tender for a Pina Colada cocktail. She sat down at one of the stools and took a sip of her drink. She felt his eyes burning into her skin. She knew she was tipsy and had to be careful and in control of what words came out of her mouth, but she had to know what his problem was.

"Officer friendly", she smiled, the smile reaching her playful eyes and making them shine with amusement, "What can I help you with?"

He looked around the room and then took the seat next to her, "My name is Detective Leon Kingston for the…"

"Rivervalle police department", she stated looking directly at him, "Is there something I need to know about?"

"How do you know me?"

"I've seen you around Leon. You were in the second year above me at school. I recognised the hair and, I saw you at the station when I gave my report", But she also recognised him from Leanne. She'd had a major crush on him when they were younger at school. She had lied to many a guy and gal stating that he was her boyfriend, but funnily enough, he never took interest in her, which for

Death's Carousel

Leanne must have been a huge blow to her ego, then she noticed Tristan, of course she got her claws into her Tristan. *Ah how things may have been different if she had snared Leon instead? If she had let Kayella and Tristan be together instead… Maybe… Just maybe they might all still be alive… Maybe!*

He looked her deadpan in the eyes, his handsome and deep grey blue eyes searching hers, his mousey brown hair was cut into a mid-fade kind of crew cut, that was shorter on the sides but longer on top and front, it framed his face with a kind of fringe type thing going on. It flopped and moved when he moved, it was shiny and had natural golden highlights running through it. Just her type… Her new type…

"I worked on the case of the Riverside murders yes", he said.

"You mean the Carousel Killers", she corrected him.

He nodded, his hair bobbing with the movement, god she wanted to run her hands through that hair, "Yes, sorry for the incorrect statement".

"Ok…And?" She asked taking another sip.

"I suspect there is some form of… Foul play there. I don't think all the killers were killed… I think there is still one left…", he said, his eyes staring into hers.

She kept hers looking into his, they didn't shift or falter, just stayed the same, giving nothing away, "Oh, is that so Mr Kingston? Do we have any idea whom? Is there anything I can help with at all?"

He watched her for a moment before retrieving his phone and pulling up a couple of photo's, "These mean anything to you?"

She looked, one was of an engagement ring, but it had been, taken apart, "Er... A broken ring?"

"It was found by Tristan", he replied flatly.

She nodded, "Ok, but I'm unsure why you think that concerns me? Didn't Leanne have an affair? Maybe he took her ring away from her?"

"Leanne still had her engagement on, it had... Melted to her fingers in the fires", he said.

Kayella swallowed, trying not to show any emotion other than that of false sympathy, "Oh, my, that's just... So... Upsetting".

"Do you know of any reason why he might have a second ring?" He asked, his cold eyes pouring into hers, reading her every flicker of emotion.

"No, we weren't that close as friends. I mean, yeah, they invited me to their party but... I wasn't close to any of them, not really. Maybe he had an affair too?" She tried to throw him under the bus, even though he was dead now didn't mean she wouldn't use him to get away with all these murders.

"And does this mean anything to you?" He swiped the phone's screen revealing a long shard of glass, it was blackened with spots of blood, and a delicately carved 'K'. The same shard she had used to pierce his soul, his body...

Her heart hammered in her chest, but she tried to play it cool, act confused. As she spoke to Leon, she couldn't help but think about, *how Tristan, even after death was trying to get to her, to take back his words of forgiveness!*

"I… I don't know why a 'K' is there?" She said, licking her lips.

Leon nodded, "You sure? It seems like a message of sorts".

She knew he would keep pressing her, she had to give him something, plus he had been there, been around when the others had bullied her, been there at the bouncy castle party, where Tristan had pulled her from the pool, to stop her drowning, where mere moments before they had been walking around talking, "Me and Tristan were close once, before him and Leanne started dating but… When him and Leanne got close, I pulled back from the group. They did invite me to the party, maybe he… felt bad… I dunno?" She tried to sound so sincere, so truthful.

He stared into her eyes, trying to read anything, before looking away, clearly, he was upset by her not giving him anything, she gave him things he already knew, but nothing incriminating.

"Are you insinuating that I had something to do with this?" She asked, sounding, upset, offended, hurt, feigning it all.

"Not yet… But I'm working on it".

There was an awkward silence between them for a moment before she broke the tension, "It's weird because the main Detective called and said the case was basically closed due to the evidence. And you, weren't you one of the main Detectives too?"

He nodded, "I was…"

"But?" She pressed.

"I have reason to believe that not all the evidence is as it seems", He replied.

"Oh... Right", she took another sip of her drink. She laughed inside a fearful laugh, but it made her feel alive, but she remained calm on the outside, she juts had to play it cool, play it well, there was nothing to incriminate her, she had made sure of that... Just because Tristan had Scratched a 'K' into glass meant nothing. It could just be a message to her to apologise, or to say well done, you won, you didn't come to the party.

"Well, if I can help at all in any way, Leon... Let me know". She could feel it, a spark, some form of interest and not just because he suspected her of... Something. But there was a clear, interest between them both but she desperately wanted to pull back from this conversation, she needed to be back in control, not him.

He studied her, and yet she studied him back, "I'll be in touch Miss Kennedy".

"Please call me Kayella", she smiled, "You want a cocktail, my treat?"

He paused mulling it over, either because he actually wanted to or more because he was clearly wondering if getting her drunk would cause her to spill the beans, but it would not, she was in control, no one else. "No best not whilst I'm on duty".

"On duty? But this is not your jurisdiction officer?" She stated but asking it as a question.

"It wasn't but it is now, I requested a transfer", he replied.

This time she couldn't help letting puzzlement flash in her eyes. *A transfer? Was that even a thing and so*

Death's Carousel

quickly? Maybe he was lying or maybe he was undercover investigating her. Whatever the reason she had to play it cool, she had to be calm and not give anything away. Make it so his so called 'Transfer' was a waste of time… but maybe she could still have a little fun. So, she ran along with it, "I'm confused. I mean, first up congratulations on the transfer, Los Angeles is so much nicer in weather than Rivervalle, am I right? But what does that have to do with me? If the officers back home need my assistance, they have my contact details, and my agents details too, I'm not going anywhere and even if I did my face is plastered on everything at the moment… Where would I run to? And that glass thing, could it just be coincidence? How do you not know that it had been graffitied before, and he just happened to use the one with it on?"

He smiled, amusement now crossing over his eyes, "Yes, they would contact you, but I am running my own private investigation… I feel there is more to this story and you, are not telling us everything you know! But I'm going to be sticking around for if you wish to share", he paused, "And coincidence? He took out a diamond from a ring and used it to send a message, with a 'K'… You are a 'K'".

She took a large swig of her cocktail and placed the glass down on the bar, she toyed with the rim of the cocktail glass, looking over at him and his boyish good looks, "If I had anything to share, I would have already… But", she paused licking a drop of lone alcohol that sat on her lip, "If you wish to come see me some time, you can. Be nice to know someone from home around here, I'd hate to be lonely and all on my lonesome… And maybe we can talk".

"Talk about the 'K'?" He pushed. "Well, how about now?"

"Am I under obligation to talk now? Maybe I should consult my Lawyer first?" She purred, teasing.

He leaned back, frustration crossing his handsome features, "Or maybe we talk now, off the record".

"Is that meant to make me feel better? Like you're not trying to frame me for something I didn't do? Maybe Leon… That 'K' means nothing, maybe it was their way of saying they were the killer, no one else…"

"Maybe… Or maybe it is connected to you?"

"Or maybe not…" She eyed him playfully, telling him with her eyes he was getting nothing out of her, "Maybe I'm just a nice girl that you should sit and have a drink with and not question about traumatic events".

He sat still for a moment trying to read her, their eyes locking on to one another, "Maybe some other time Miss Kennedy, see you around". He rose from his seat and went to walk off.

"Wait", she said making him pause. She grabbed a serviette and scribbled down her hotel and room number, "Take this", she passed it to him, "You might need it".

He took it biting his lip. She wanted those lips to be hers, all hers, she wanted to be greedy and have them all to herself, kissing her own. She could feel a fiery passion burn in her, a need, a lust, just for him. It could be mutual attraction or just simply the alcohol and the high from her career boost from the talk show, or maybe just a thrill of danger but she didn't care as to why, she just wanted him.

"Like I said, see you around Miss… Kayella", he finished and then walked off to the door.

Death's Carousel

"See you around indeed", she muttered to herself. *There was no way a police officer would just transfer here on a hunch, right? That sounded like movie type shit? Maybe... Someone had hired him as a private investigator? Both Tristan and Leanne's families had money... Maybe just maybe they suspected the foul play? Or it was lies?*

She stayed sat for a moment, her heart hammering in her chest. *What on earth did he think he knew? Was it something bad? Could it incriminate her?*

Ordering another drink and downing it in seconds she decided the party was over and she called for a driver to come and collect her and to drop her off at her hotel that was a few streets away.

*

Back at her hotel she put her key in the lock and let herself into her room. She took of her heels that had made her feet ache, she rubbed them trying to get the feeling back into them. As she went to unzip her dress a knock on the door caught her attention. Looking around the room she searched for a weapon, it was early hours of the morning, who on earth would be calling at this hour, not room service that was for sure and her agents and PR team were all still out partying.

Nothing came to mind so she grabbed a heel, a stiletto heel to the face could still do some damage if need be.

She opened the door and gasped, officer friendly was standing there, changed from his uniform, his casual shirt not buttoned up fully, the top button was open and revealed a silky-smooth chest that she wanted to feel and touch. A midnight blue bomber jacket showed of his broad muscular build. He wore denim jeans and white Nike trainers.

She put on a big smile, "Well, Leon what brings you here?"

"It's officer Kingston to you", he replied.

She couldn't tell if he was being serious or not, so she reached out a hand and placed it on his chest, "Did you come here thinking you could sleep with me to get some information?" It was a bold statement and very forward, but she was feeling bold, her new life was just beginning, and she didn't want to be the quiet little lamb anymore. And she wanted him, and she wanted him now.

She thought he might be taken a back by her boldness, but instead he smiled, "Maybe".

Her grin widened, "Well, I have no information for you Leon… But… Maybe I could use the company tonight".

He waivered for a moment, unsure. She could tell her boldness, and willingness to allow him in had thrown him. Surely someone hiding secrets wouldn't let someone of the law in so freely and easily.

She rubbed her hand down his chest, pulling gently at his shirt. The motion seemed to make up his mind and he followed her into her room. Closing the door behind her she dropped her stiletto to the floor, looking deeply into his eyes before jumping up onto him. She wrapped her arms round his shoulders and her legs round his waist, pulling him ever closer to her.

Death's Carousel

Their eyes read into each other, both trying to steal secrets from one another but neither giving anything away. She could tell Leon was dangerous too, something about him gave off that energy… *Maybe he was someone who's energy could match her own? He had in the past blown off Leanne, her nemesis, that meant they had something in common… A Dislike…*

She smiled, a girly, seductive smile, she knew this was dangerous, she knew this was playing with fire, but something burned within her, a need to feel the thrill of the danger.

Shaking her hair from side to side, letting it fall around him like a long dark curtain she placed her lips on his. The heat of the moment and passion burst through them both like an electrical current, like the one that had danced through Sinead and Mario. The adrenaline from the memory tore through her body and she kissed him harder.

"What are you waiting for?" She said, her voice breaking with the need. The need for a new thrill to take over from the old one, it was like an addiction, a drug. She was addicted to danger and the thrill of nearly being caught.

He carried her to the bedroom and closed the door with one elbow.

It was hard to breathe beneath the sheets and he and Kayella made new music for her body to dance to. The thrill of the deadly fire licking at her senses. As they danced well into the morning, she knew she had found a new play mate, a new dangerous playmate that could either fulfil her new wildest dreams or destroy them in a heartbeat, *but that was the thrill of it right? A thrill to keep her mind occupied and not thinking about what would fill the empty void, the void where the plan for revenge used to thrive and drive her…*

Revenge was all the fun at the fair, but danger was a type of ecstasy, a drug, something that kept calling to her time and time again, round and round like a Carousel, and it was all fun and pain. She would have the fun and deliver the pain to those who deserved it…

Maybe her list would grow again… But for now, revenge was sleeping with the guy that Leanne had wanted her whole school life and beyond to get with. And now he was all Kayella's, she was like a black widow watching their mate, ready to kill and eat when the time was right… But for now, her web of lies and deception would hold. She wanted to enjoy this moment, to enjoy life and she was most certainly looking forward to her tour that she was preparing for which would start very soon and finish in just under a year… On the anniversary of those she killed at the fun fair and on Death's Carousel…

The End… Or is it?

Death's Carousel

Song Book...

*Death's Carousel...

Merry-Go-Round, Merry-Go-Round, on a carousel, the dead go.

Merry-Go-Round, Merry-Go-Round, on a carousel, the dead know.

Running away won't get you far, in this nightmare, but you can try.

Merry-Go-Round, Merry-Go-Round, on a carousel... The dead show...

Merry, Merry-Go-Round, Merry, Merry-Go-Round, Merry, Merry-Go-Round.

Come ride the Thestral, the horse of death, on this carousel, don't lose your breath, come take deaths hand, so you'll understand, why you're here, at the Merry-Go-Round... Round... You go.

And it's all fun and pain, this is deaths game,
One of you will die, and you won't make it off the ride, so try, try to run and hide.

Merry-Go-Round, Merry-Go-Round, on a carousel, the dead go.

Merry-Go-Round, Merry-Go-Round, on a carousel, the dead know.

Running away won't get you far, in this nightmare tale, but you can try.

Death's Carousel

Are you too stupid and slow, how can you not know?
What you, what you…did! To me…eeee…
I'm not a freak, how dared you speak.
You tore my soul, but now your souls on show.

And it's all fun and pain, this is deaths game.
One of you will die, and you won't make it off the ride, so try, try to run and hide.

Merry-Go-Round, Merry-Go-Round, on a carousel, the dead go.
Merry-Go-Round, Merry-Go-Round, on a carousel, the dead know.
Running away won't get you far, in this nightmare, but you can try.
Merry-Go-Round, Merry-Go-Round, on a carousel… The dead show…

Why did you hate me?
And you had no heart?
You had no reason,
To make the chaos start,
My life was ruined.
And torn apart.
But now I've grown and I'm powerful.
So now… It's your turn, your turn, your turn… To die! Or at least try… Not too…

Merry-Go-Round, Merry-Go-Round, on a carousel, the dead go.

Piper Nuelle

Merry-Go-Round, Merry-Go-Round, on a carousel, the dead know.

Running away won't get you far, in this nightmare, but you can try.

Merry-Go-Round, Merry-Go-Round, on deaths carousel... The dead show

Written by Kayella Kennedy... Inspired by Nancy Fairweather...

Death's Carousel

* Sorry, Not, Sorry...

Sorry, not sorry for what I did,
You were going to rat me out to my secret love that I hid,
Sorry, not sorry I don't want no peace,
There will be no olive branch from this mouthpiece.
Sorry, not sorry for what I said,
Test me again and you will be dead.
Sorry, not sorry, that your done in the head,
Being friends with you gave me no street cred.
The Carousel torture was just a start,
Because you saw into my true heart.
I will get revenge for me being grounded,
I will make sure that your head will be pounded.
Running away won't get you far…
But you can try, you can try, you can try, try, try!!

Written by Nancy Fairweather and adapted to song by Kayella Kennedy.

*Bouncy Razor Castle...

Bouncy Razor Castle,
Bouncy Razor Castle,
Why did I get an invite here?
Now my blood is all over the party bags,
Tell me why that everyone is here?
Is it so they can poke and sneer, at me now?

Maybe this is a prank for me?
Again now, Again now,
Maybe the name Skank for me,
Is not the worst now, the worst now.

Chorus x 2
It's a castle, a bouncy razor castle,
And I'll bleed if you make me, bleed, bleed, bleed,
Let's bring out the cake and blow the candles out,
I need help and I'm shouting out with doubt...

Wrap me up and open me like a present,
Your all Lords and Ladies, and I'm the peasant,
Tell me why the bunting drips with blood,
Is it because mine is mud now?

Maybe this is a prank for me?
Again now, Again now,
Maybe the name Skank for me,
Is not the worst now, the worst now.

Death's Carousel

Chorus x 2
It's a castle, a bouncy razor castle,
And I'll bleed if you make me, bleed, bleed, bleed,
Let's bring out the cake and blow the candles out,
I need help and I'm washed with doubt.

Bridge x 3
I'm bleeding, I'm dying, you're killing me, I'm crying…

It's a castle, a bouncy razor castle,
And I'll bleed if you make me, bleed, bleed, bleed,
Let's bring out the cake and blow the candles out,
I need help and I'm shouting out with doubt…

It's a castle, a bouncy razor castle,
It's a castle, a bouncy…Razor…Castle…

Written by Kayella Kennedy… Inspired by Sinead Wilson…

Piper Nuelle

* Porta-Loo Playdate

Porta-Loo-ooooooo,
Porta-Loo-ooooooo.

You messaged me a playdate,
So, I came to your home,
Theres's others there that came to play,
But they leave me alone.
You tell them, oh the poor freak,
She just wants to play,
But truly, really, I don't want to stay.

Your playin, playin spin the bottle,
Let's go full throttle on the freakazoid,
Ahh, Ahh… Loo…
She's a freak, so she has no feeling,
Spin it to the ceiling, to the Porta-Loo.

You don't give a shit about our friendship now,
You'd rather be plastic like your loo,
You grab my head and pull me down,
You flush the water of the Porta-Loo.

Porta-Loo-ooooooo,
Porta-Loo-ooooooo,

Coughing, choking, poison, burning my lungs,
Trying to breathe, this shit water isn't fun,
When I try to talk to you, my words don't make hit,
This playdate, is burning like hells pit,

Death's Carousel

This playdate is so boring,
Now that you're whoring,
In your Porta-Loo.

Your playin, playin spin the bottle,
Let's go full throttle, on the freakazoid,
Porta- Loo-oooooooo,
She's a freak, so she has no feeling,
Spin it to the ceiling, to the Porta-Loo-oooooooo.

You don't give a shit about our friendship now,
You'd rather be plastic like your loo,
You grab my head and push me down,
You flush the water of the Porta-Loo.

Flush it down, Flush it down, you flush it so I cannot scream,
Flush it down, Flush it down, you're going to fall apart at the seams.

I don't give a shit about our friendship now,
I'm gonna be plastic just like you,
I'm gonna grab your head and push you down,
I'm gonna flush the shit out of you!

Written by Kayella Kennedy... Inspired by Mariella Coppard...

* Whack a Mole Boy...

Whack a mole, Whack a boy,
Whack a mole, Whack a boy,

Piper Nuelle

Whack a mole, Whack a boy,

Always aiming the hammer at me,
As your fist hit me down, down, down,
You lift it again at me,
So, you can hit your final blow, blow, blow.
You're a guy,
but you think it's cool to pick on a girl, girl, girl,
All for a girl,
That you make her hurl, hurl, hurl.
If you dangle the hammer one more time, time, time,
It'll end up where the sun doesn't shine, shine, shine.

I know my strength inside,
Is more than yours outside,
I say whack a mole, whack a mole boy,
You think your stronger than me,
But I have to disagree,
Whack a mole, whack a mole boy.

I'm not that little girl now, now, now,
Who's scared to go and tell now, now, now,
I will show you power now, now, now,
Little whack a mole boy,
You won the fight back then how, how, how,
With your fist pow, pow, pow,
But I will fight back now, now, now,
Little whack a mole boy.

Whack a mole, whack a mole boy,
Whack a mole, whack a mole boy,

Death's Carousel

Whack a mole, whack a mole boy,
Whack a boy, ah, ah, Whack a boy.

Hammers aren't always appropriate weapons,
Sometimes all that's needed is one perfect word,
You punch and kick and spit at me,
Just to impress some girl,
But you're not her boyfriend,
And she doesn't want you,
The perfect word is… Revenge…

I know my strength inside,
Is more than yours outside,
I say whack a mole, Whack a mole boy,
You think your stronger than me,
But I have to disagree,
Whack a mole, whack a mole boy,

I'm not a little girl now, now, now,
Who's scared to go and tell now, now, now,
Little whack a mole boy,
You won the fight back then how, how, how,
With your fist pow, pow, pow,
But I will fight back now, now, now,
Little whack a mole boy.

Whack a mole, Whack a mole boy,
Whack a mole, Whack a mole boy,
Whack a mole, Whack a mole boy,
Oh, whack a mole boy…

Piper Nuelle

I'm not that little girl now, now, now,
Who's scared to go and tell now, now, now,
I will show you power now, now, now,
Little whack a mole boy,
You won the fight back then how, how, how,
With your fists pow, pow, pow,
But I will fight back now,
Little whack a mole boy.

Ahh, Ahh, Whack a mole boy,
Ahh, Ahh, Whack a mole boy,
Ahh, Ahh, Whack a mole…
Boy…

Written by Kayella Kennedy… Inspired by Mario Coppard…

Death's Carousel

* Bumper Car Tag, Dodgem Hide and Seek...

Riding in your daddy's Audi,
You pulled up to me, said Howdy,
I like you think your real dead cute,
Can't tell my friends or they'll execute,
Me...
Speeding in the multistorey,
Things about to get really gory,
You have no license to thrill,
But I have a license to kill...You...

Bumping cars in the car park,
It's late, It's getting pretty dark,
Bumper car tag, Dodgem hide and seek,
Not getting kidnapped is looking pretty bleak,
Pushed the throttle, pulled the choke,
You dragged me off in a cloud of smoke,
Bumper car tag, Dodgem hide and seek,
You lock me in the boot, so I cannot speak,
Tyres screaming, tyres screeching, Vibrating in the sky,
Electricity powering as the dodgems fly,
Bumper car tag, Dodgem hide and seek...

Cotton candy hangs in the air,
We would make a real great pair,
Secrecy to hide our relationship,
If they find out, I'll have no friendship.

Bumping cars in the park,

Piper Nuelle

It's late, It's getting pretty dark,
Other than the metal spark,
Bumper car tag, Dodgem hide and seek,
Pushed the throttle, pulled the choke,
You dragged me off in a cloud of smoke,
Bumper car tag, Dodgem hide and seek,
Tyres screaming, tyres screeching, vibrating in the sky,
Electricity powering as the dodgems fly,
I will smile as I watch you fry,
Bumper car tag, Dodgem hide and seek.

Bumper car tag, Dodgem hide and seek,
Bumper car tag, Dodgem hide and seek,
And now I seek you out, my fire and rage pour out the spout.

Fire burning, scalding me,
As I'm trying to break free,
If she flees just let her be,
Fire burning, scalding you,
As your trying to break free,
As you flee, I won't let you be,
I'll repeat what you did to me,
Bumper car tag,
Dodgem hide and seek…

Bumping cars in the car park…
It's late, It's getting pretty dark…
Bumper car tag, Dodgem hide and seek…

Written by Kayella Kennedy… Inspired by Luke Godden…

Death's Carousel

* Punch and Judy...

Punch and Judy their strung,
Puppets for the puppeteer on string,
A professor, a teacher of violence,
No need to take offence,
Getting high on glue, till their lips turn blue,
Putting pins on seats, till my blood runs true,
Their laughter like voices of a Kazoo-oooo.

Judy peels glue from her face,
Stuck together, Outlines to trace,
Punch peels glue from his face,
Stuck together, Outlines to trace.

Bikini photos from the beach,
Edited so people can leech,
Stuck to the school with glue,
I will never live this through,
I'm not a prude, But damn girl they look nude,
And now everyone is being so rude,
Even the teachers, Now being Leech-ers,
My bodies a pin up, a seaside cone cup,
Punch wants to lick me, Judy wants to kick me.

Punch me and kick me, Judy, Judy does hate me,
My pictures are scattered,
With pins and glue, now back to you.

Judy peels glue from her face,
Stuck together, Outlines to trace,

Piper Nuelle

Punch peels glue from his face,
Stuck together, Outlines to trace.

The puppeteer now moves you,
You dance to my tune,
In the theatre box,
I pull the strings and close the locks,
I stuck you together, in hell you both belong,
As you dance to my deathly song.

The glue shall pair,
Making you as one,
My revenge has only just begun,
And now it seems I have won,
Punch wants to lick me, Judy wants to kick me.

You say I'm crazy, You wouldn't be wrong,
I wasn't born a bitch, People like you made me itch.
I say you're crazy too, Cause you started this,
But I'm the crazy bitch, that will finish it…

Judy peels glue from her face,
Stuck together, Outlines to trace,
Punch peels glue from his face,
Stuck together, Outlines to trace…

Written by Kayella Kennedy… Inspired by Jared Knight and Leanne McBride…

Death's Carousel

* House of Shards...

Mirror, Mirror who's the sharpest of them all?

Think I just remembered something,
The mirror reflected it to me,
Like a clear looking glass,
A river of memories,
A Crystal ball,
Who is the fairest of them all?

I look into the mirror, I quiver, at the person I see right now, It shatters all over the floor,
    Oh no, it smashes, oh well,
    Seven years bad luck don't seem swell,
    Who's the sharpest of them all?

I see the reflection of me, she's been couped up,
She wishes to be free, Mirror, Mirror, Mirror of me,
I see the reflection of you, And everything you put me through, Mirror, Mirror, Mirror of you.

I think our world in crumbling,
I think I'm spiralling and tumbling,
Down a giant rabbit hole,
Through a mirrored void, I fall…
I wish I could stand and be tall,
But the mirror image of me is cracking up.

I look into the mirror, I quiver, at the person I see right now, It shatters all over the floor,

Piper Nuelle

Oh no, It smashes, oh well, Seven years bad luck don't seem so swell, Who's the sharpest of them all?

I see the reflection of me, She's been couped up,
She wishes to be free, Mirror, Mirror, Mirror of me,
I see the reflection of you, and everything you put me through, Mirror, Mirror, Mirror of you...

I see the reflection of me, She's been couped up,
She wishes to be free, Mirror, mirror, mirror of me,
I see the reflection of you, and everything you put me through, Mirror...Mirror...Mirror...Of...You...

Written by Kayella Kennedy... Inspired by Leanne McBride...

Death's Carousel

Playlist...

Here is the playlist that I listened to when writing this book, the songs are all Melanie Martinez songs and inspired a lot of my ideas and my basis for my main character Kayella. I wanted her to be edgy and cool like Melanie but I've also added in a lot of trauma so people can see why my main character is and becomes the villain... If you haven't already, make sure you check out Melanie Martinez and her music, it is amazing!!! And I love her way of storytelling through music, it's so compelling and unique. Plus, me and my littlest munchkin may have gone to see her in concert for her Trilogy Tour in London back in 2024... Which maybe inspiring my next story for Kayella!!!

- Soap – Melanie Martinez – Cry Baby
- Pacify Her – Melanie Martinez – Cry Baby
- Cry Baby – Melanie Martinez – Cry Baby
- Carousel – Melanie Martinez – Cry Baby
- Alphabet Boy – Melanie Martinez – Cry Baby
- Pity Party – Melanie Martinez – Cry Baby
- Tag, You're It – Melanie Martinez – Cry Baby
- Dollhouse – Melanie Martinez – Cry Baby
- Mad Hatter – Melanie Martinez – Cry Baby
- Play Date – Melanie Martinez – Cry Baby
- Death – Melanie Martinez – Portals
- Void – Melanie Martinez – Portals
- Tunnel Vision – Melanie Martinez – Portals
- Battle of the Larynx – Melanie Martinez – Portals

Disclaimer – Whilst the story and the songs have been inspired by a musical artist I admire because I listened to them whilst I wrote, the book and its story and all its contents are all my own idea and was an idea I'd had written down many years ago, but I left it alone for a long time, because I didn't know how to process it into written words. But, from one artist to another I will give credit where credit is due, and inspiration did come to me through Melanie Martinez's music, and I will always be a huge fan of her work. Plus, she got my daughter out of a very dark and difficult time, she was there for her when no one else was. And for that, I will be forever eternally thankful and grateful.

Xo Piper Xo

Death's Carousel

Piper Nuelle

Death's Carousel

Piper Nuelle

Printed in Dunstable, United Kingdom